MANIFESTO OF THE COMMUNIST PARTY

AND

MINUTES OF THE SECOND CONGRESS OF THE COMMUNIST INTERNATIONAL

Karl Marx

MANIFESTO OF THE COMMUNIST PARTY

BY

KARL MARX AND FRIEDRICH ENGELS

AND

MINUTES
OF THE
SECOND CONGRESS
OF THE
COMMUNIST INTERNATIONAL

BY

V. I. LENIN

CLASSIC
PUBLISHED BY

SEAWOLF
PRESS

MANIFESTO

OF THE

COMMUNIST PARTY

BY

KARL MARX and FRIEDRICH ENGELS

A SPECTRE is haunting Europe—the spectre of Communism. All the Powers of old Europe have entered into a holy alliance to exorcise this spectre: Pope and Czar, Metternich and Guizot, French Radicals and German police-spies.

Where is the party in opposition that has not been decried as Communistic by its opponents in power? Where is the Opposition that has not hurled back the branding reproach of Communism, against the more advanced opposition parties, as well as against its reactionary adversaries?

Two things result from this fact.

I. Communism is already acknowledged by all European Powers to be itself a Power.

II. It is high time that Communists should openly, in the face of the whole world, publish their views, their aims, their tendencies, and meet this nursery tale of the Spectre of Communism with a Manifesto of the party itself.

To this end, Communists of various nationalities have assembled in London, and sketched the following Manifesto, to be published in the English, French, German, Italian, Flemish and Danish languages.

I.

BOURGEOIS AND PROLETARIANS

The history of all hitherto existing societies is the history of class struggles.

Freeman and slave, patrician and plebeian, lord and serf, guild-master and journeyman, in a word, oppressor and oppressed, stood in constant opposition to one another, carried on an uninterrupted, now hidden, now open fight, a fight that each time ended, either in a revolutionary re-constitution of society at large, or in the common ruin of the contending classes.

In the earlier epochs of history, we find almost everywhere a complicated arrangement of society into various orders, a manifold gradation of social rank. In ancient Rome we have patricians, knights, plebeians, slaves; in the Middle Ages, feudal lords, vassals, guild-masters, journeymen, apprentices, serfs; in almost all of these classes, again, subordinate gradations.

The modern bourgeois society that has sprouted from the ruins of feudal society has not done away with class antagonisms. It has but established new classes, new conditions of oppression, new forms of struggle in place of the old ones. Our epoch, the epoch of the bourgeoisie, possesses, however, this distinctive feature: it has simplified the class antagonisms. Society as a whole is more and more splitting up into two great hostile camps, into two great classes, directly facing each other: Bourgeoisie and Proletariat.

From the serfs of the Middle Ages sprang the chartered burghers of the earliest towns. From these burgesses the first elements of the bourgeoisie were developed.

The discovery of America, the rounding of the Cape, opened up fresh ground for the rising bourgeoisie. The East-Indian and Chinese markets, the colonization of America, trade with the colonies, the increase in the means of exchange and in commodities generally, gave to commerce, to navigation, to industry, an impulse never before known, and thereby, to the revolutionary element in the tottering feudal society, a rapid development.

The feudal system of industry, under which industrial production was monopolized by closed guilds, now no longer sufficed for the growing wants of the new markets. The manufacturing system took its place. The guild-masters were pushed on one side by the manufacturing middle class; division of labor between the different corporate guilds vanished in the face of division of labor in each single workshop.

Meantime the markets kept ever growing, the demand ever rising. Even manufacture no longer sufficed. Thereupon, steam and machinery revolutionized industrial production. The place of manufacture was taken by the giant, Modern Industry, the place of the industrial middle class, by industrial millionaires, the leaders of whole industrial armies, the modern bourgeois.

Modern industry has established the world-market, for which the discovery of America paved the way. This market has given an immense development to commerce, to navigation, to communication by land. This development has, in its time, reacted on the extension of industry; and in proportion as industry, commerce, navigation, railways extended, in the same proportion the bourgeoisie developed, increased its capital, and pushed into the background every class handed down from the Middle Ages.

We see, therefore, how the modern bourgeoisie is itself the product of a long course of development, of a series of revolutions in the modes of production and of exchange.

Each step in the development of the bourgeoisie was accompanied by a corresponding political advance of that class. An oppressed class under the sway of the feudal nobility, an armed and self-governing association in the mediaeval commune; here independent urban republic (as in Italy and Germany), there taxable "third estate" of the monarchy (as in France), afterwards, in the period of manufacture proper, serving either the semi-feudal or the absolute monarchy as a counterpoise against the nobility, and, in fact, corner-stone of the great monarchies in general, the bourgeoisie has at last, since the establishment of Modern Industry and of the world-market, conquered for itself, in the modern representative State, exclusive political sway. The executive of the modern State is but a committee for managing the common affairs of the whole bourgeoisie.

The bourgeoisie, historically, has played a most revolutionary part.

The bourgeoisie, wherever it has got the upper hand, has put an end to all feudal, patriarchal, idyllic relations. It has pitilessly torn asunder the motley feudal ties that bound man to his "natural superiors," and has left remaining no other nexus between man and man than naked self-interest, than callous "cash payment." It has drowned the most heavenly ecstasies of religious fervor, of chivalrous enthusiasm, of philistine sentimentalism, in the icy water of egotistical calculation. It has resolved personal worth into exchange value, and in place of the numberless and indefeasible chartered freedoms, has set up that single, unconscionable freedom—Free Trade. In one word, for exploitation, veiled by religious and political illusions, naked, shameless, direct, brutal exploitation.

The bourgeoisie has stripped of its halo every occupation hitherto honored and looked up to with reverent awe. It has converted the physician, the lawyer, the priest, the poet, the man of science, into its paid wage laborers.

The bourgeoisie has torn away from the family its sentimental veil, and has reduced the family relation to a mere money relation.

The bourgeoisie has disclosed how it came to pass that the brutal display of vigor in the Middle Ages, which Reactionists so much admire, found its fitting complement in the most slothful indolence. It has been the first to show what man's activity can bring about. It has accomplished wonders far surpassing Egyptian pyramids, Roman aqueducts, and Gothic cathedrals; it has conducted expeditions that put in the shade all former Exoduses of nations and crusades.

The bourgeoisie cannot exist without constantly revolutionizing the instruments of production, and thereby the relations of production, and with them the whole relations of society. Conservation of the old modes of production in unaltered form, was, on the contrary, the first condition of existence for all earlier industrial classes. Constant revolutionizing of production, uninterrupted disturbance of all social conditions, everlasting uncertainty and agitation distinguish the bourgeois epoch from all earlier ones. All fixed, fast-frozen relations, with their train of ancient and venerable prejudices and opinions, are swept away, all new-formed ones become antiquated before they can ossify. All that is solid melts into air, all that is holy is profaned, and man is at last compelled to face with sober senses, his real conditions of life, and his relations with his kind.

The need of a constantly expanding market for its products chases the bourgeoisie over the whole surface of the globe. It must nestle everywhere, settle everywhere, establish connexions everywhere.

The bourgeoisie has through its exploitation of the world-market given a cosmopolitan character to production and consumption in every country. To the great chagrin of Reactionists, it has drawn from under the feet of industry the national ground on which it stood. All old-established national industries have been destroyed or are daily being destroyed. They are dislodged by new industries, whose introduction becomes a life and death question for all civilised nations, by industries that no longer work up indigenous raw material, but raw material drawn from the remotest zones; industries whose products are consumed, not only at home, but in every quarter of the globe. In place of the old wants, satisfied by the productions of the country, we find new wants, requiring for their satisfaction the products of distant lands and climes. In place of the old local and national seclusion and self-sufficiency, we have intercourse in every direction, universal inter-dependence of nations. And as in material, so also in intellectual production. The intellectual creations of individual nations become common property. National one-sidedness and narrow-mindedness become more and more impossible, and from the numerous national and local literatures, there arises a world literature.

The bourgeoisie, by the rapid improvement of all instruments of production, by the immensely facilitated means of communication, draws all, even the most barbarian, nations into civilization. The cheap prices of its commodities are the heavy artillery with which it batters down all Chinese walls, with which it forces the barbarians' intensely obstinate hatred of foreigners to capitulate. It compels all nations, on pain of extinction, to adopt the bourgeois mode of production; it compels them to introduce what it calls civilization into their midst, i.e., to become bourgeois themselves. In one word, it creates a world after its own image.

The bourgeoisie has subjected the country to the rule of the towns. It has created enormous cities, has greatly increased the urban population as compared with the rural, and has thus rescued a considerable part of the population from the idiocy of rural life. Just as it has made the country dependent on the towns, so it has made barbarian and semi-barbarian countries dependent on the civilised ones, nations of peasants on nations of bourgeois, the East on the West.

The bourgeoisie keeps more and more doing away with the scattered state of the population, of the means of production, and of property. It has agglomerated production, and has concentrated property in a few hands. The necessary consequence of this was political centralisation. Independent, or but loosely connected provinces, with separate interests, laws, governments and systems of taxation, became lumped together into one nation, with one government, one code of laws, one national class-interest, one frontier and one customs-tariff. The bourgeoisie, during its rule of scarce one hundred years, has created more massive and more colossal productive forces than have all preceding generations together. Subjection of Nature's forces to man, machinery, application of chemistry to industry and agriculture, steam-navigation, railways, electric telegraphs, clearing of whole continents for cultivation, canalization of rivers, whole populations conjured out of the ground—what earlier century had even a presentiment that such productive forces slumbered in the lap of social labor?

We see then: the means of production and of exchange, on whose foundation the bourgeoisie built itself up, were generated in feudal society. At a certain stage in the development of these means of production and of exchange, the conditions under which feudal society produced and exchanged, the feudal organization of agriculture and manufacturing industry, in one word, the feudal relations of property became no longer compatible with the already developed productive forces; they became so many fetters. They had to be burst asunder; they were burst asunder.

Into their place stepped free competition, accompanied by a social and political constitution adapted to it, and by the economical and political sway of the bourgeois class.

A similar movement is going on before our own eyes. Modern bourgeois society with its relations of production, of exchange and of property, a society that has conjured up such gigantic means of production and of exchange, is like the sorcerer, who is no longer able to control the powers of the nether world whom he has called up by his spells. For many a decade past the history of industry and commerce is but the history of the revolt of modern productive forces against modern conditions of production, against the property relations that are the conditions for the existence of the bourgeoisie and of its rule. It is enough to mention the commercial crises that by their periodical return put on its trial, each time more threateningly, the existence of the entire bourgeois society. In these crises a great part not only of the existing products, but also of the previously created productive forces, are periodically destroyed. In these crises there breaks out an epidemic that, in all earlier epochs, would have seemed an absurdity—the epidemic of over-production. Society suddenly finds itself put back into a state of momentary barbarism; it appears as if a famine, a universal war of devastation had cut off the supply of every means of subsistence; industry and commerce seem to be destroyed; and why? Because there is too much civilization, too much means of subsistence, too much industry, too much commerce. The productive forces at the disposal of society no longer tend to further the development of the conditions of bourgeois property; on the contrary, they have become too powerful for these conditions, by which they are fettered, and so soon as they overcome these fetters, they bring disorder into the whole of bourgeois society, endanger the existence of bourgeois property. The conditions of bourgeois society are too narrow to comprise the wealth created by them. And how does the bourgeoisie get over these crises? On the one hand enforced destruction of a mass of productive forces; on the other, by the conquest of new markets, and by the more thorough exploitation of the old ones. That is to say, by paving the way for more extensive and more destructive crises, and by diminishing the means whereby crises are prevented.

The weapons with which the bourgeoisie felled feudalism to the ground are now turned against the bourgeoisie itself.

But not only has the bourgeoisie forged the weapons that bring death to itself; it has also called into existence the men who are to wield those weapons—the modern working class—the proletarians.

In proportion as the bourgeoisie, i.e., capital, is developed, in the same proportion is the proletariat, the modern working class, developed—a class of laborers, who live only so long as they find work, and who find work only so long as their labor increases capital. These laborers, who must sell themselves piece-meal, are a commodity, like every other article of commerce, and are consequently exposed to all the vicissitudes of competition, to all the fluctuations of the market.

Owing to the extensive use of machinery and to division of labor, the work of the proletarians has lost all individual character, and consequently, all charm for the workman. He becomes an appendage of the machine, and it is only the most simple, most monotonous, and most easily acquired knack, that is required of him. Hence, the cost of production of a workman is restricted, almost entirely, to the means of subsistence that he requires for his maintenance, and for the propagation of his race. But the price of a commodity, and therefore also of labor, is equal to its cost of production. In proportion therefore, as the repulsiveness of the work increases, the wage decreases. Nay more, in proportion as the use of machinery and division of labor increases, in the same proportion the burden of toil also increases, whether by prolongation of the working hours, by increase of the work exacted in a given time or by increased speed of the machinery, etc.

Modern industry has converted the little workshop of the patriarchal master into the great factory of the industrial capitalist. Masses of laborers, crowded into the factory, are organized like soldiers. As privates of the industrial army they are placed under the command of a perfect hierarchy of officers and sergeants. Not only are they slaves of the bourgeois class, and of the bourgeois State; they are daily and hourly enslaved by the machine, by the over-looker, and, above all, by the individual bourgeois manufacturer himself. The more openly this despotism proclaims gain to be its end and aim, the more petty, the more hateful and the more embittering it is.

The less the skill and exertion of strength implied in manual labor, in other words, the more modern industry becomes developed, the more is the labor of men superseded by that of women. Differences of age and sex have no longer any distinctive social validity for the working class. All are instruments of labor, more or less expensive to use, according to their age and sex.

No sooner is the exploitation of the laborer by the manufacturer, so far at an end, that he receives his wages in cash, than he is set upon by the other portions of the bourgeoisie, the landlord, the shopkeeper, the pawnbroker, etc.

The lower strata of the middle class—the small tradespeople, shopkeepers, retired tradesmen generally, the handicraftsmen and peasants—all these sink gradually into the proletariat, partly because their diminutive capital does not suffice for the scale on which Modern Industry is carried on, and is swamped in the competition with the large capitalists, partly because their specialized skill is rendered worthless by the new methods of production. Thus the proletariat is recruited from all classes of the population.

The proletariat goes through various stages of development. With its birth begins its struggle with the bourgeoisie. At first the contest is carried on by individual laborers, then by the workpeople of a factory, then by the operatives of one trade, in one locality, against the individual bourgeois who directly exploits them. They direct their attacks not against the bourgeois conditions of production, but against the instruments of production themselves; they destroy imported wares that compete with their labor, they smash to pieces machinery, they set factories ablaze, they seek to restore by force the vanished status of the workman of the Middle Ages.

At this stage the laborers still form an incoherent mass scattered over the whole country, and broken up by their mutual competition. If anywhere they unite to form more compact bodies, this is not yet the consequence of their own active union, but of the union of the bourgeoisie, which class, in order to attain its own political ends, is compelled to set the whole proletariat in motion, and is moreover yet, for a time, able to do so. At this stage, therefore, the proletarians do not fight their enemies, but the enemies of their enemies, the remnants of absolute monarchy, the landowners, the non-industrial bourgeois, the petty bourgeoisie. Thus the whole historical movement is concentrated in the hands of the bourgeoisie; every victory so obtained is a victory for the bourgeoisie.

But with the development of industry the proletariat not only increases in number; it becomes concentrated in greater masses, its strength grows, and it feels that strength more. The various interests and conditions of life within the ranks of the proletariat are more and more equalized, in proportion as machinery obliterates all distinctions of labor, and nearly everywhere reduces wages to the same low level. The growing competition among the bourgeois, and the resulting commercial crises, make the wages of the workers ever more fluctuating. The unceasing improvement of machinery, ever more rapidly developing, makes their livelihood more and more precarious; the collisions between individual workmen and individual bourgeois take more and more the character of collisions between two classes. Thereupon the workers begin to form combinations (Trades Unions) against the bourgeois; they club together in order to keep up the rate of wages; they found permanent associations in order to make provision beforehand for these occasional revolts. Here and there the contest breaks out into riots.

Now and then the workers are victorious, but only for a time. The real fruit of their battles lies, not in the immediate result, but in the ever-expanding union of the workers. This union is helped on by the improved means of communication that are created by modern industry and that place the workers of different localities in contact with one another. It was just this contact that was needed to centralise the numerous local struggles, all of the same character, into one national struggle between classes. But every class struggle is a political struggle. And that union, to attain which the burghers of the Middle Ages, with their miserable highways, required centuries, the modern proletarians, thanks to railways, achieve in a few years.

This organization of the proletarians into a class, and consequently into a political party, is continually being upset again by the competition between the workers themselves. But it ever rises up again, stronger, firmer, mightier. It compels legislative recognition of particular interests of the workers, by taking advantage of the divisions among the bourgeoisie itself. Thus the ten-hours' bill in England was carried.

Altogether collisions between the classes of the old society further, in many ways, the course of development of the proletariat. The bourgeoisie finds itself involved in a constant battle. At first with the aristocracy; later on, with those portions of the bourgeoisie itself, whose interests have become antagonistic to the progress of industry; at all times, with the bourgeoisie of foreign countries. In all these battles it sees itself compelled to appeal to the proletariat, to ask for its help, and thus, to drag it into the political arena. The bourgeoisie itself, therefore, supplies the proletariat with its own instruments of political and general education, in other words, it furnishes the proletariat with weapons for fighting the bourgeoisie.

Further, as we have already seen, entire sections of the ruling classes are, by the advance of industry, precipitated into the proletariat, or are at least threatened in their conditions of existence. These also supply the proletariat with fresh elements of enlightenment and progress.

Finally, in times when the class struggle nears the decisive hour, the process of dissolution going on within the ruling class, in fact within the whole range of society, assumes such a violent, glaring character, that a small section of the ruling class cuts itself adrift, and joins the revolutionary class, the class that holds the future in its hands. Just as, therefore, at an earlier period, a section of the nobility went over to the bourgeoisie, so now a portion of the bourgeoisie goes over to the proletariat, and in particular, a portion of the bourgeois ideologists, who have raised themselves to the level of comprehending theoretically the historical movement as a whole.

Of all the classes that stand face to face with the bourgeoisie today, the proletariat alone is a really revolutionary class. The other classes decay and finally disappear in the face of Modern Industry; the proletariat is its special and essential product. The lower middle class, the small manufacturer, the shopkeeper, the artisan, the peasant, all these fight against the bourgeoisie, to save from extinction their existence as fractions of the middle class. They are therefore not revolutionary, but conservative. Nay more, they are reactionary, for they try to roll back the wheel of history. If by chance they are revolutionary, they are so only in view of their impending transfer into the proletariat, they thus defend not their present, but their future interests, they desert their own standpoint to place themselves at that of the proletariat.

The "dangerous class," the social scum, that passively rotting mass thrown off by the lowest layers of old society, may, here and there, be swept into the movement by a proletarian revolution; its conditions of life, however, prepare it far more for the part of a bribed tool of reactionary intrigue.

In the conditions of the proletariat, those of old society at large are already virtually swamped. The proletarian is without property; his relation to his wife and children has no longer anything in common with the bourgeois family-relations; modern industrial labor, modern subjection to capital, the same in England as in France, in America as in Germany, has stripped him of every trace of national character. Law, morality, religion, are to him so many bourgeois prejudices, behind which lurk in ambush just as many bourgeois interests.

All the preceding classes that got the upper hand, sought to fortify their already acquired status by subjecting society at large to their conditions of appropriation. The proletarians cannot become masters of the productive forces of society, except by abolishing their own previous mode of appropriation, and thereby also every other previous mode of appropriation. They have nothing of their own to secure and to fortify; their mission is to destroy all previous securities for, and insurances of, individual property.

All previous historical movements were movements of minorities, or in the interests of minorities. The proletarian movement is the self-conscious, independent movement of the immense majority, in the interests of the immense majority. The proletariat, the lowest stratum of our present society, cannot stir, cannot raise itself up, without the whole superincumbent strata of official society being sprung into the air.

Though not in substance, yet in form, the struggle of the proletariat with the bourgeoisie is at first a national struggle. The proletariat of each country must, of course, first of all settle matters with its own bourgeoisie.

In depicting the most general phases of the development of the proletariat, we traced the more or less veiled civil war, raging within existing society, up to the point where that war breaks out into open revolution, and where the violent overthrow of the bourgeoisie lays the foundation for the sway of the proletariat.

Hitherto, every form of society has been based, as we have already seen, on the antagonism of oppressing and oppressed classes. But in order to oppress a class, certain conditions must be assured to it under which it can, at least, continue its slavish existence. The serf, in the period of serfdom, raised himself to membership in the commune, just as the petty bourgeois, under the yoke of feudal absolutism, managed to develop into a bourgeois. The modern laborer, on the contrary, instead of rising with the progress of industry, sinks deeper and deeper below the conditions of existence of his own class. He becomes a pauper, and pauperism develops more rapidly than population and wealth. And here it becomes evident, that the bourgeoisie is unfit any longer to be the ruling class in society, and to impose its conditions of existence upon society as an over-riding law. It is unfit to rule because it is incompetent to assure an existence to its slave within his slavery, because it cannot help letting him sink into such a state, that it has to feed him, instead of being fed by him. Society can no longer live under this bourgeoisie, in other words, its existence is no longer compatible with society.

The essential condition for the existence, and for the sway of the bourgeois class, is the formation and augmentation of capital; the condition for capital is wage-labor. Wage-labor rests exclusively on competition between the laborers. The advance of industry, whose involuntary promoter is the bourgeoisie, replaces the isolation of the laborers, due to competition, by their revolutionary combination, due to association. The development of Modern Industry, therefore, cuts from under its feet the very foundation on which the bourgeoisie produces and appropriates products. What the bourgeoisie, therefore, produces, above all, is its own grave-diggers. Its fall and the victory of the proletariat are equally inevitable.

II.

PROLETARIANS AND COMMUNISTS

In what relation do the Communists stand to the proletarians as a whole?

The Communists do not form a separate party opposed to other working-class parties.

They have no interests separate and apart from those of the proletariat as a whole.

They do not set up any sectarian principles of their own, by which to shape and mould the proletarian movement.

The Communists are distinguished from the other working-class parties by this only: (1) In the national struggles of the proletarians of the different countries, they point out and bring to the front the common interests of the entire proletariat, independently of all nationality. (2) In the various stages of development which the struggle of the working class against the bourgeoisie has to pass through, they always and everywhere represent the interests of the movement as a whole.

The Communists, therefore, are on the one hand, practically, the most advanced and resolute section of the working-class parties of every country, that section which pushes forward all others; on the other hand, theoretically, they have over the great mass of the proletariat the advantage of clearly understanding the line of march, the conditions, and the ultimate general results of the proletarian movement.

The immediate aim of the Communist is the same as that of all the other proletarian parties: formation of the proletariat into a class, overthrow of the bourgeois supremacy, conquest of political power by the proletariat.

The theoretical conclusions of the Communists are in no way based on ideas or principles that have been invented, or discovered, by this or that would-be universal reformer. They merely express, in general terms, actual relations springing from an existing class struggle, from a historical movement going on under our very eyes. The abolition of existing property relations is not at all a distinctive feature of Communism.

All property relations in the past have continually been subject to historical change consequent upon the change in historical conditions.

The French Revolution, for example, abolished feudal property in favor of bourgeois property.

The distinguishing feature of Communism is not the abolition of property generally, but the abolition of bourgeois property. But modern bourgeois private property is the final and most complete expression of the system of producing and appropriating products, that is based on class antagonisms, on the exploitation of the many by the few.

In this sense, the theory of the Communists may be summed up in the single sentence: Abolition of private property.

We Communists have been reproached with the desire of abolishing the right of personally acquiring property as the fruit of a man's own labor, which property is alleged to be the groundwork of all personal freedom, activity and independence.

Hard-won, self-acquired, self-earned property! Do you mean the property of the petty artisan and of the small peasant, a form of property that preceded the bourgeois form? There is no need to abolish that; the development of industry has to a great extent already destroyed it, and is still destroying it daily.

Or do you mean modern bourgeois private property?

But does wage-labor create any property for the laborer? Not a bit. It creates capital, i.e., that kind of property which exploits wage-labor, and which cannot increase except upon condition of begetting a new supply of wage-labor for fresh exploitation. Property, in its present form, is based on the antagonism of capital and wage-labor. Let us examine both sides of this antagonism.

To be a capitalist, is to have not only a purely personal, but a social status in production. Capital is a collective product, and only by the united action of many members, nay, in the last resort, only by the united action of all members of society, can it be set in motion.

Capital is, therefore, not a personal, it is a social power.

When, therefore, capital is converted into common property, into the property of all members of society, personal property is not thereby transformed into social property. It is only the social character of the property that is changed. It loses its class-character.

Let us now take wage-labor.

The average price of wage-labor is the minimum wage, i.e., that quantum of the means of subsistence, which is absolutely requisite in bare existence as a laborer. What, therefore, the wage-laborer appropriates by means of his labor, merely suffices to prolong and reproduce a bare existence. We by no means intend to abolish this personal appropriation of the products of labor, an appropriation that is made for the maintenance and reproduction of human life, and that leaves no surplus wherewith to command the labor of others. All that we want to do away with, is the miserable character of this appropriation, under which the laborer lives merely to increase capital, and is allowed to live only in so far as the interest of the ruling class requires it.

In bourgeois society, living labor is but a means to increase accumulated labor. In Communist society, accumulated labor is but a means to widen, to enrich, to promote the existence of the laborer.

In bourgeois society, therefore, the past dominates the present; in Communist society, the present dominates the past. In bourgeois society capital is independent and has individuality, while the living person is dependent and has no individuality.

And the abolition of this state of things is called by the bourgeois, abolition of individuality and freedom! And rightly so. The abolition of bourgeois individuality, bourgeois independence, and bourgeois freedom is undoubtedly aimed at.

By freedom is meant, under the present bourgeois conditions of production, free trade, free selling and buying.

But if selling and buying disappears, free selling and buying disappears also. This talk about free selling and buying, and all the other "brave words" of our bourgeoisie about freedom in general, have a meaning, if any, only in contrast with restricted selling and buying, with the fettered traders of the Middle Ages, but have no meaning when opposed to the Communistic abolition of buying and selling, of the bourgeois conditions of production, and of the bourgeoisie itself.

You are horrified at our intending to do away with private property. But in your existing society, private property is already done away with for nine-tenths of the population; its existence for the few is solely due to its non-existence in the hands of those nine-tenths. You reproach us, therefore, with intending to do away with a form of property, the necessary condition for whose existence is the non-existence of any property for the immense majority of society.

In one word, you reproach us with intending to do away with your property. Precisely so; that is just what we intend.

From the moment when labor can no longer be converted into capital, money, or rent, into a social power capable of being monopolized, i.e., from the moment when individual property can no longer be transformed into bourgeois property, into capital, from that moment, you say individuality vanishes.

You must, therefore, confess that by "individual" you mean no other person than the bourgeois, than the middle-class owner of property. This person must, indeed, be swept out of the way, and made impossible.

Communism deprives no man of the power to appropriate the products of society; all that it does is to deprive him of the power to subjugate the labor of others by means of such appropriation.

It has been objected that upon the abolition of private property all work will cease, and universal laziness will overtake us.

According to this, bourgeois society ought long ago to have gone to the dogs through sheer idleness; for those of its members who work, acquire nothing, and those who acquire anything, do not work. The whole of this objection is but another expression of the tautology: that there can no longer be any wage-labor when there is no longer any capital.

All objections urged against the Communistic mode of producing and appropriating material products, have, in the same way, been urged against the Communistic modes of producing and appropriating intellectual products. Just as, to the bourgeois, the disappearance of class property is the disappearance of production itself, so the disappearance of class culture is to him identical with the disappearance of all culture.

That culture, the loss of which he laments, is, for the enormous majority, a mere training to act as a machine.

But don't wrangle with us so long as you apply, to our intended abolition of bourgeois property, the standard of your bourgeois notions of freedom, culture, law, etc. Your very ideas are but the outgrowth of the conditions of your bourgeois production and bourgeois property, just as your jurisprudence is but the will of your class made into a law for all, a will, whose essential character and direction are determined by the economical conditions of existence of your class.

The selfish misconception that induces you to transform into eternal laws of nature and of reason, the social forms springing from your present mode of production and form of property—historical relations that rise and disappear in the progress of production—this misconception you share with every ruling class that has preceded you. What you see clearly in the case of ancient property, what you admit in the case of feudal property, you are of course forbidden to admit in the case of your own bourgeois form of property.

Abolition of the family! Even the most radical flare up at this infamous proposal of the Communists.

On what foundation is the present family, the bourgeois family, based? On capital, on private gain. In its completely developed form this family exists only among the bourgeoisie. But this state of things finds its complement in the practical absence of the family among the proletarians, and in public prostitution.

The bourgeois family will vanish as a matter of course when its complement vanishes, and both will vanish with the vanishing of capital.

Do you charge us with wanting to stop the exploitation of children by their parents? To this crime we plead guilty.

But, you will say, we destroy the most hallowed of relations, when we replace home education by social.

And your education! Is not that also social, and determined by the social conditions under which you educate, by the intervention, direct or indirect, of society, by means of schools, etc.? The Communists have not invented the intervention of society in education; they do but seek to alter the character of that intervention, and to rescue education from the influence of the ruling class.

The bourgeois clap-trap about the family and education, about the hallowed co-relation of parent and child, becomes all the more disgusting, the more, by the action of Modern Industry, all family ties among the proletarians are torn asunder, and their children transformed into simple articles of commerce and instruments of labor.

But you Communists would introduce community of women, screams the whole bourgeoisie in chorus.

The bourgeois sees in his wife a mere instrument of production. He hears that the instruments of production are to be exploited in common, and, naturally, can come to no other conclusion than that the lot of being common to all will likewise fall to the women.

He has not even a suspicion that the real point is to do away with the status of women as mere instruments of production.

For the rest, nothing is more ridiculous than the virtuous indignation of our bourgeois at the community of women which, they pretend, is to be openly and officially established by the Communists. The Communists have no need to introduce community of women; it has existed almost from time immemorial.

Our bourgeois, not content with having the wives and daughters of their proletarians at their disposal, not to speak of common prostitutes, take the greatest pleasure in seducing each other's wives.

Bourgeois marriage is in reality a system of wives in common and thus, at the most, what the Communists might possibly be reproached with, is that they desire to introduce, in substitution for a hypocritically concealed, an openly legalized community of women. For the rest, it is self-evident that the abolition of the present system of production must bring with it the abolition of the community of women springing from that system, i.e., of prostitution both public and private.

The Communists are further reproached with desiring to abolish countries and nationality.

The working men have no country. We cannot take from them what they have not got. Since the proletariat must first of all acquire political supremacy, must rise to be the leading class of the nation, must constitute itself the nation, it is, so far, itself national, though not in the bourgeois sense of the word.

National differences and antagonisms between peoples are daily more and more vanishing, owing to the development of the bourgeoisie, to freedom of commerce, to the world-market, to uniformity in the mode of production and in the conditions of life corresponding thereto.

The supremacy of the proletariat will cause them to vanish still faster. United action, of the leading civilised countries at least, is one of the first conditions for the emancipation of the proletariat.

In proportion as the exploitation of one individual by another is put an end to, the exploitation of one nation by another will also be put an end to. In proportion as the antagonism between classes within the nation vanishes, the hostility of one nation to another will come to an end.

The charges against Communism made from a religious, a philosophical, and, generally, from an ideological standpoint, are not deserving of serious examination.

Does it require deep intuition to comprehend that man's ideas, views and conceptions, in one word, man's consciousness, changes with every change in the conditions of his material existence, in his social relations and in his social life?

What else does the history of ideas prove, than that intellectual production changes its character in proportion as material production is changed? The ruling ideas of each age have ever been the ideas of its ruling class.

When people speak of ideas that revolutionize society, they do but express the fact, that within the old society, the elements of a new one have been created, and that the dissolution of the old ideas keeps even pace with the dissolution of the old conditions of existence.

When the ancient world was in its last throes, the ancient religions were overcome by Christianity. When Christian ideas succumbed in the 18th century to rationalist ideas, feudal society fought its death battle with the then revolutionary bourgeoisie. The ideas of religious liberty and freedom of conscience merely gave expression to the sway of free competition within the domain of knowledge.

"Undoubtedly," it will be said, "religious, moral, philosophical and juridical ideas have been modified in the course of historical development. But religion, morality philosophy, political science, and law, constantly survived this change."

"There are, besides, eternal truths, such as Freedom, Justice, etc. that are common to all states of society. But Communism abolishes eternal truths, it abolishes all religion, and all morality, instead of constituting them on a new basis; it therefore acts in contradiction to all past historical experience."

What does this accusation reduce itself to? The history of all past society has consisted in the development of class antagonisms, antagonisms that assumed different forms at different epochs.

But whatever form they may have taken, one fact is common to all past ages, viz., the exploitation of one part of society by the other. No wonder, then, that the social consciousness of past ages, despite all the multiplicity and variety it displays, moves within certain common forms, or general ideas, which cannot completely vanish except with the total disappearance of class antagonisms.

The Communist revolution is the most radical rupture with traditional property relations; no wonder that its development involves the most radical rupture with traditional ideas.

But let us have done with the bourgeois objections to Communism.

We have seen above, that the first step in the revolution by the working class, is to raise the proletariat to the position of ruling as to win the battle of democracy.

The proletariat will use its political supremacy to wrest, by degrees, all capital from the bourgeoisie, to centralise all instruments of production in the hands of the State, i.e., of the proletariat organized as the ruling class; and to increase the total of productive forces as rapidly as possible.

Of course, in the beginning, this cannot be effected except by means of despotic inroads on the rights of property, and on the conditions of bourgeois production; by means of measures, therefore, which appear economically insufficient and untenable, but which, in the course of the movement, outstrip themselves, necessitate further inroads upon the old social order, and are unavoidable as a means of entirely revolutionizing the mode of production.

These measures will of course be different in different countries.

Nevertheless in the most advanced countries, the following will be pretty generally applicable.

1. Abolition of property in land and application of all rents of land to public purposes.

2. A heavy progressive or graduated income tax.

3. Abolition of all right of inheritance.

4. Confiscation of the property of all emigrants and rebels.

5. Centralisation of credit in the hands of the State, by means of a national bank with State capital and an exclusive monopoly.

6. Centralisation of the means of communication and transport in the hands of the State.

7. Extension of factories and instruments of production owned by the State; the bringing into cultivation of wastelands, and the improvement of the soil generally in accordance with a common plan.

8. Equal liability of all to labor. Establishment of industrial armies, especially for agriculture.

9. Combination of agriculture with manufacturing industries; gradual abolition of the distinction between town and country, by a more equable distribution of the population over the country.

10. Free education for all children in public schools. Abolition of children's factory labor in its present form. Combination of education with industrial production, &c., &c.

When, in the course of development, class distinctions have disappeared, and all production has been concentrated in the hands of a vast association of the whole nation, the public power will lose its political character. Political power, properly so called, is merely the organized power of one class for oppressing another. If the proletariat during its contest with the bourgeoisie is compelled, by the force of circumstances, to organize itself as a class, if, by means of a revolution, it makes itself the ruling class, and, as such, sweeps away by force the old conditions of production, then it will, along with these conditions, have swept away the conditions for the existence of class antagonisms and of classes generally, and will thereby have abolished its own supremacy as a class.

In place of the old bourgeois society, with its classes and class antagonisms, we shall have an association, in which the free development of each is the condition for the free development of all.

III.

SOCIALIST AND COMMUNIST LITERATURE

1. Reactionary Socialism
a. Feudal Socialism

Owing to their historical position, it became the vocation of the aristocracies of France and England to write pamphlets against modern bourgeois society. In the French revolution of July 1830, and in the English reform agitation, these aristocracies again succumbed to the hateful upstart. Thenceforth, a serious political contest was altogether out of the question. A literary battle alone remained possible. But even in the domain of literature the old cries of the restoration period had become impossible.

In order to arouse sympathy, the aristocracy were obliged to lose sight, apparently, of their own interests, and to formulate their indictment against the bourgeoisie in the interest of the exploited working class alone. Thus the aristocracy took their revenge by singing lampoons on their new master, and whispering in his ears sinister prophecies of coming catastrophe.

In this way arose Feudal Socialism: half lamentation, half lampoon; half echo of the past, half menace of the future; at times, by its bitter, witty and incisive criticism, striking the bourgeoisie to the very heart's core; but always ludicrous in its effect, through total incapacity to comprehend the march of modern history.

The aristocracy, in order to rally the people to them, waved the proletarian alms-bag in front for a banner. But the people, so often as it joined them, saw on their hindquarters the old feudal coats of arms, and deserted with loud and irreverent laughter.

One section of the French Legitimists and "Young England" exhibited this spectacle.

In pointing out that their mode of exploitation was different to that of the bourgeoisie, the feudalists forget that they exploited under circumstances and conditions that were quite different, and that are now antiquated. In showing that, under their rule, the modern proletariat never existed, they forget that the modern bourgeoisie is the necessary offspring of their own form of society.

For the rest, so little do they conceal the reactionary character of their criticism that their chief accusation against the bourgeoisie amounts to this, that under the bourgeois regime a class is being developed, which is destined to cut up root and branch the old order of society.

What they upbraid the bourgeoisie with is not so much that it creates a proletariat, as that it creates a revolutionary proletariat.

In political practice, therefore, they join in all coercive measures against the working class; and in ordinary life, despite their high falutin phrases, they stoop to pick up the golden apples dropped from the tree of industry, and to barter truth, love, and honor for traffic in wool, beetroot-sugar, and potato spirits.

As the parson has ever gone hand in hand with the landlord, so has Clerical Socialism with Feudal Socialism.

Nothing is easier than to give Christian asceticism a Socialist tinge. Has not Christianity declaimed against private property, against marriage, against the State? Has it not preached in the place of these, charity and poverty, celibacy and mortification of the flesh, monastic life and Mother

Church? Christian Socialism is but the holy, water with which the priest consecrates the heart-burnings of the aristocrat.

B. Petty-Bourgeois Socialism

The feudal aristocracy was not the only class that was ruined by the bourgeoisie, not the only class whose conditions of existence pined and perished in the atmosphere of modern bourgeois society. The mediaeval burgesses and the small peasant proprietors were the precursors of the modern bourgeoisie. In those countries which are but little developed, industrially and commercially, these two classes still vegetate side by side with the rising bourgeoisie.

In countries where modern civilization has become fully developed, a new class of petty bourgeois has been formed, fluctuating between proletariat and bourgeoisie and ever renewing itself as a supplementary part of bourgeois society. The individual members of this class, however, are being constantly hurled down into the proletariat by the action of competition, and, as modern industry develops, they even see the moment approaching when they will completely disappear as an independent section of modern society, to be replaced, in manufactures, agriculture and commerce, by overlookers, bailiffs and shopmen.

In countries like France, where the peasants constitute far more than half of the population, it was natural that writers who sided with the proletariat against the bourgeoisie, should use, in their criticism of the bourgeois regime, the standard of the peasant and petty bourgeois, and from the standpoint of these intermediate classes should take up the cudgels for the working class. Thus arose petty-bourgeois Socialism. Sismondi was the head of this school, not only in France but also in England.

This school of Socialism dissected with great acuteness the contradictions in the conditions of modern production. It laid bare the hypocritical apologies of economists. It proved, incontrovertibly, the disastrous effects of machinery and division of labor; the concentration of capital and land in a few hands; overproduction and crises; it pointed out the inevitable ruin of the petty bourgeois and peasant, the misery of the proletariat, the anarchy in production, the crying inequalities in the distribution of wealth, the industrial war of extermination between nations, the dissolution of old moral bonds, of the old family relations, of the old nationalities.

In its positive aims, however, this form of Socialism aspires either to restoring the old means of production and of exchange, and with them the old property relations, and the old society, or to cramping the modern means of production and of exchange, within the framework of the old property relations that have been, and were bound to be, exploded by those means. In either case, it is both reactionary and Utopian.

Its last words are: corporate guilds for manufacture, patriarchal relations in agriculture.

Ultimately, when stubborn historical facts had dispersed all intoxicating effects of self-deception, this form of Socialism ended in a miserable fit of the blues.

C. German, or "True," Socialism

The Socialist and Communist literature of France, a literature that originated under the pressure of a bourgeoisie in power, and that was the expression of the struggle against this power, was introduced into Germany at a time when the bourgeoisie, in that country, had just begun its contest with feudal absolutism.

German philosophers, would-be philosophers, and beaux esprits, eagerly seized on this literature, only forgetting, that when these writings immigrated from France into Germany, French social conditions had not immigrated along with them. In contact with German social conditions, this French literature lost all its immediate practical significance, and assumed a purely literary aspect. Thus, to the German philosophers of the eighteenth century, the demands of the first French Revolution were nothing more than the demands of "Practical Reason" in general, and the utterance of the will of the revolutionary French bourgeoisie signified in their eyes the law of pure Will, of Will as it was bound to be, of true human Will generally.

The world of the German literate consisted solely in bringing the new French ideas into harmony with their ancient philosophical conscience, or rather, in annexing the French ideas without deserting their own philosophic point of view.

This annexation took place in the same way in which a foreign language is appropriated, namely, by translation.

It is well known how the monks wrote silly lives of Catholic Saints over the manuscripts on which the classical works of ancient heathendom had been written. The German literate reversed this process with the profane French literature. They wrote their philosophical nonsense beneath the French original. For instance, beneath the French criticism of the economic functions of money, they wrote "Alienation of Humanity," and beneath the French criticism of the bourgeois State they wrote "dethronement of the Category of the General," and so forth.

The introduction of these philosophical phrases at the back of the French historical criticisms they dubbed "Philosophy of Action," "True Socialism," "German Science of Socialism," "Philosophical Foundation of Socialism," and so on.

The French Socialist and Communist literature was thus completely emasculated. And, since it ceased in the hands of the German to express the struggle of one class with the other, he felt conscious of having overcome "French one-sidedness" and of representing, not true requirements, but the requirements of truth; not the interests of the proletariat, but the interests of Human Nature, of Man in general, who belongs to no class, has no reality, who exists only in the misty realm of philosophical fantasy.

This German Socialism, which took its schoolboy task so seriously and solemnly, and extolled its poor stock-in-trade in such mountebank fashion, meanwhile gradually lost its pedantic innocence.

The fight of the German, and especially, of the Prussian bourgeoisie, against feudal aristocracy and absolute monarchy, in other words, the liberal movement, became more earnest.

By this, the long wished-for opportunity was offered to "True" Socialism of confronting the political movement with the Socialist demands, of hurling the traditional anathemas against liberalism, against representative government, against bourgeois competition, bourgeois freedom of the press, bourgeois legislation, bourgeois liberty and equality, and of preaching to the masses that they had nothing to gain, and everything to lose, by this bourgeois movement. German Socialism forgot, in the nick of time, that the French criticism, whose silly echo it was, presupposed the existence of modern bourgeois society, with its corresponding economic conditions of existence, and the political constitution adapted thereto, the very things whose attainment was the object of the pending struggle in Germany.

To the absolute governments, with their following of parsons, professors, country squires and officials, it served as a welcome scarecrow against the threatening bourgeoisie.

It was a sweet finish after the bitter pills of floggings and bullets with which these same governments, just at that time, dosed the German working-class risings.

While this "True" Socialism thus served the governments as a weapon for fighting the German bourgeoisie, it, at the same time, directly represented a reactionary interest, the interest of the German Philistines. In Germany the petty-bourgeois class, a relic of the sixteenth century, and since then constantly cropping up again under various forms, is the real social basis of the existing state of things.

To preserve this class is to preserve the existing state of things in Germany. The industrial and political supremacy of the bourgeoisie threatens it with certain destruction; on the one hand, from the concentration of capital; on the other, from the rise of a revolutionary proletariat. "True" Socialism appeared to kill these two birds with one stone. It spread like an epidemic.

The robe of speculative cobwebs, embroidered with flowers of rhetoric, steeped in the dew of sickly sentiment, this transcendental robe in which the German Socialists wrapped their sorry "eternal truths," all skin and bone, served to wonderfully increase the sale of their goods amongst such a public. And on its part, German Socialism recognized, more and more, its own calling as the bombastic representative of the petty-bourgeois Philistine.

It proclaimed the German nation to be the model nation, and the German petty Philistine to be the typical man. To every villainous meanness of this model man it gave a hidden, higher, Socialistic interpretation, the exact contrary of its real character. It went to the extreme length of directly opposing the "brutally destructive" tendency of Communism, and of proclaiming its supreme and impartial contempt of all class struggles. With very few exceptions, all the so-called Socialist and Communist publications that now (1847) circulate in Germany belong to the domain of this foul and enervating literature.

----

2. Conservative, or Bourgeois, Socialism

A part of the bourgeoisie is desirous of redressing social grievances, in order to secure the continued existence of bourgeois society.

To this section belong economists, philanthropists, humanitarians, improvers of the condition of the working class, organizers of charity, members of societies for the prevention of cruelty to animals, temperance fanatics, hole-and-corner reformers of every imaginable kind. This form of Socialism has, moreover, been worked out into complete systems.

We may cite Proudhon's *Philosophie de la Misere* as an example of this form.

The Socialistic bourgeois want all the advantages of modern social conditions without the struggles and dangers necessarily resulting therefrom. They desire the existing state of society minus its revolutionary and disintegrating elements. They wish for a bourgeoisie without a proletariat. The bourgeoisie naturally conceives the world in which it is supreme to be the best; and bourgeois Socialism develops this comfortable conception into various more or less complete systems. In requiring the proletariat to carry out such a system, and thereby to march straightway into the social New Jerusalem, it but requires in reality, that the proletariat should remain within the bounds of existing society, but should cast away all its hateful ideas concerning the bourgeoisie.

A second and more practical, but less systematic, form of this Socialism sought to depreciate every revolutionary movement in the eyes of the working class, by showing that no mere political reform, but only a change in the material conditions of existence, in economic relations, could be of any advantage to them. By changes in the material conditions of existence, this form of Socialism, however, by no means understands abolition of the bourgeois relations of production, an abolition that can be effected only by a revolution, but administrative reforms, based on the continued existence of these relations; reforms, therefore, that in no respect affect the relations between capital and labor, but, at the best, lessen the cost, and simplify the administrative work, of bourgeois government.

Bourgeois Socialism attains adequate expression, when, and only when, it becomes a mere figure of speech.

Free trade: for the benefit of the working class. Protective duties: for the benefit of the working class. Prison Reform: for the benefit of the working class. This is the last word and the only seriously meant word of bourgeois Socialism.

It is summed up in the phrase: the bourgeois is a bourgeois—for the benefit of the working class.

3. Critical-Utopian Socialism and Communism

We do not here refer to that literature which, in every great modern revolution, has always given voice to the demands of the proletariat, such as the writings of Babeuf and others.

The first direct attempts of the proletariat to attain its own ends, made in times of universal excitement, when feudal society was being overthrown, these attempts necessarily failed, owing to the then undeveloped state of the proletariat, as well as to the absence of the economic conditions for its emancipation, conditions that had yet to be produced, and could be produced by the impending bourgeois epoch alone. The revolutionary literature that accompanied these first movements of the proletariat had necessarily a reactionary character. It inculcated universal asceticism and social levelling in its crudest form.

The Socialist and Communist systems properly so called, those of Saint-Simon, Fourier, Owen and others, spring into existence in the early undeveloped period, described above, of the struggle between proletariat and bourgeoisie (see Section 1. Bourgeois and Proletarians).

The founders of these systems see, indeed, the class antagonisms, as well as the action of the decomposing elements, in the prevailing form of society. But the proletariat, as yet in its infancy, offers to them the spectacle of a class without any historical initiative or any independent political movement.

Since the development of class antagonism keeps even pace with the development of industry, the economic situation, as they find it, does not as yet offer to them the material conditions for the emancipation of the proletariat. They therefore search after a new social science, after new social laws, that are to create these conditions.

Historical action is to yield to their personal inventive action, historically created conditions of emancipation to fantastic ones, and the gradual, spontaneous class-organization of the proletariat to the organization of society specially contrived by these inventors. Future history resolves itself, in their eyes, into the propaganda and the practical carrying out of their social plans.

In the formation of their plans they are conscious of caring chiefly for the interests of the working class, as being the most suffering class. Only from the point of view of being the most suffering class does the proletariat exist for them.

The undeveloped state of the class struggle, as well as their own surroundings, causes Socialists of this kind to consider themselves far superior to all class antagonisms. They want to improve the condition of every member of society, even that of the most favoured. Hence, they habitually appeal to society at large, without distinction of class; nay, by preference, to the ruling class. For how can people, when once they understand their system, fail to see in it the best possible plan of the best possible state of society?

Hence, they reject all political, and especially all revolutionary, action; they wish to attain their ends by peaceful means, and endeavour, by small experiments, necessarily doomed to failure, and by the force of example, to pave the way for the new social Gospel.

Such fantastic pictures of future society, painted at a time when the proletariat is still in a very undeveloped state and has but a fantastic conception of its own position correspond with the first instinctive yearnings of that class for a general reconstruction of society.

But these Socialist and Communist publications contain also a critical element. They attack every principle of existing society. Hence they are full of the most valuable materials for the enlightenment of the working class. The practical measures proposed in them—such as the abolition of the distinction between town and country, of the family, of the carrying on of industries for the account of private individuals, and of the wage system, the proclamation of social harmony, the conversion of the functions of the State into a mere superintendence of production, all these proposals, point solely to the disappearance of class antagonisms which were, at that time, only just cropping up, and which, in these publications, are recognized in their earliest, indistinct and undefined forms only. These proposals, therefore, are of a purely Utopian character.

The significance of Critical-Utopian Socialism and Communism bears an inverse relation to historical development. In proportion as the modern class struggle develops and takes definite shape, this fantastic standing apart from the contest, these fantastic attacks on it, lose all practical value and all theoretical justification. Therefore, although the originators of these systems were, in many respects, revolutionary, their disciples have, in every case, formed mere reactionary sects. They hold fast by the original views of their masters, in opposition to the progressive historical development of the proletariat. They, therefore, endeavour, and that consistently, to deaden the class struggle and to reconcile the class antagonisms. They still dream of experimental realization of their social Utopias, of founding isolated "phalansteres," of establishing "Home Colonies," of setting up a "Little Icaria"—duodecimo editions of the New Jerusalem—and to realize all these castles in the air, they are compelled to appeal to the feelings and purses of the bourgeois. By degrees they sink into the category of the reactionary conservative Socialists depicted above, differing from these only by more systematic pedantry, and by their fanatical and superstitious belief in the miraculous effects of their social science.

They, therefore, violently oppose all political action on the part of the working class; such action, according to them, can only result from blind unbelief in the new Gospel.

The Owenites in England, and the Fourierists in France, respectively, oppose the Chartists and the "Reformistes."

IV.

POSITION OF THE COMMUNISTS IN RELATION TO THE VARIOUS EXISTING OPPOSITION PARTIES

Section II has made clear the relations of the Communists to the existing working-class parties, such as the Chartists in England and the Agrarian Reformers in America.

The Communists fight for the attainment of the immediate aims, for the enforcement of the momentary interests of the working class; but in the movement of the present, they also represent and take care of the future of that movement. In France the Communists ally themselves with the Social-Democrats, against the conservative and radical bourgeoisie, reserving, however, the right to take up a critical position in regard to phrases and illusions traditionally handed down from the great Revolution.

In Switzerland they support the Radicals, without losing sight of the fact that this party consists of antagonistic elements, partly of Democratic Socialists, in the French sense, partly of radical bourgeois.

In Poland they support the party that insists on an agrarian revolution as the prime condition for national emancipation, that party which fomented the insurrection of Cracow in 1846.

In Germany they fight with the bourgeoisie whenever it acts in a revolutionary way, against the absolute monarchy, the feudal squirearchy, and the petty bourgeoisie.

But they never cease, for a single instant, to instil into the working class the clearest possible recognition of the hostile antagonism between bourgeoisie and proletariat, in order that the German workers may straightaway use, as so many weapons against the bourgeoisie, the social and political conditions that the bourgeoisie must necessarily introduce along with its supremacy, and in order that, after the fall of the reactionary classes in Germany, the fight against the bourgeoisie itself may immediately begin.

The Communists turn their attention chiefly to Germany, because that country is on the eve of a bourgeois revolution that is bound to be carried out under more advanced conditions of European civilization, and with a much more developed proletariat, than that of England was in the seventeenth, and of France in the eighteenth century, and because the bourgeois revolution in Germany will be but the prelude to an immediately following proletarian revolution.

In short, the Communists everywhere support every revolutionary movement against the existing social and political order of things.

In all these movements they bring to the front, as the leading question in each, the property question, no matter what its degree of development at the time.

Finally, they labor everywhere for the union and agreement of the democratic parties of all countries.

The Communists disdain to conceal their views and aims. They openly declare that their ends can be attained only by the forcible overthrow of all existing social conditions. Let the ruling classes tremble at a Communistic revolution. The proletarians have nothing to lose but their chains. They have a world to win.

Working men of all countries, unite!

Minutes
of the
Second Congress
of the
Communist International[1]

V. I. Lenin

July 19-August 7, 1920

1

Report On The International Situation
And The Fundamental Tasks Of
The Communist International
July 19

[1]   The Second Congress of the Communist International met from July 19 to August 7, 1920. The opening session was held in Petrograd and the subsequent sessions in Moscow. It was attended by over 200 delegates who represented workers ' organizations of 37 countries. Apart from delegates representing the Communist parties and organizations of 31 countries, there were delegates from the Independent Social-Democratic Party of Germany, the Socialist parties of Italy and France, Industrial Workers of the World (Australia, Britain and Ireland), the National Confederation of Labor of Spain and other organizations.

Lenin directed all the preparatory work before the Congress. At its first session he made a report on the international situation and the fundamental tasks of the Communist International. Throughout the Congress, in his reports and speeches, Lenin fought uncompromisingly against the opportunist Centrist parties, who were attempting to penetrate into the Third International, and levelled sharp criticism at the anarcho-syndicalist trends and "Left" sectarianism of a number of communist organizations. Lenin took part in the work of various commissions and delivered reports and speeches on the international situation and the fundamental tasks of the Communist International, the national and the colonial questions, the agrarian question and the terms of admission into the Communist International. Lenin's theses on the fundamental tasks of the Second Congress of the Communist International, the national and the colonial questions, the agrarian question and the terms of admission into the Communist International were endorsed as Congress decisions.

The Second Congress laid the foundations of the programme, organizational principles, strategy and tactics of the Communist International;—Editor.

(*An ovation breaks out. All present rise to their feet and applaud. The speaker tries to begin, but the applause and cries in all languages continue. The ovation does not abate.*) Comrades, the theses on the questions of the fundamental tasks of the Communist International have been published in all languages and contain nothing that is materially new (particularly to the Russian comrades). That is because, in a considerable measure, they extend several of the main features of our revolutionary experience and the lessons of our revolutionary movement to a number of Western countries, to Western Europe. My report will therefore deal at greater length, if in brief outline, with the first part of my subject, namely, the international situation.

Imperialism's economic relations constitute the core of the entire international situation as it now exists. Throughout the twentieth century, this new, highest and final stage of capitalism has fully taken shape. Of course, you all know that the enormous dimensions that capital has reached are the most characteristic and essential feature of imperialism. The place of free competition has been taken by huge monopolies. An insignificant number of capitalists have, in some cases, been able to concentrate in their hands entire branches of industry; these have passed into the hands of combines, cartels, syndicates and trusts, not infrequently of an international nature. Thus, entire branches of industry, not only in single countries, but all over the world, have been taken over by monopolists in the field of finance, property rights, and partly of production. This has formed the basis for the unprecedented domination exercised by an insignificant number of very big banks, financial tycoons, financial magnates who have, in fact, transformed even the freest republics into financial monarchies. Before the war this was publicly recognized by such far from revolutionary writers as, for example, Lysis in France.

This domination by a handful of capitalists achieved full development when the whole world had been partitioned, not only in the sense that the various sources of raw materials and means of production had been seized by the biggest capitalists, but also in the sense that the preliminary partition of the colonies had been completed. Some forty years ago, the population of the colonies stood at somewhat over 250,000,000, who were subordinated to six capitalist powers. Before the war of 1914, the population of the colonies was estimated at about 600,000,000, and if we add countries like Persia, Turkey, and China, which were already semi-colonies, we shall get, in round figures, a population of a thousand million people oppressed through colonial dependence by the richest, most civilised and freest countries. And you know that, apart from direct political and juridical dependence, colonial dependence presumes a number of relations of financial and economic dependence, a number of wars, which were not regarded as wars because very often they amounted to sheer massacres, when European and American imperialist troops, armed with the most up-to-date weapons of destruction, slaughtered the unarmed and defenceless inhabitants of colonial countries.

The first imperialist war of 1914-18 was the inevitable outcome of this partition of the whole world, of this domination by the capitalist monopolies, of this great power wielded by an insignificant number of very big banks—two, three, four or five in each country. This war was waged for the repartitioning of the whole world. It was waged in order to decide which of the small groups of the biggest states—the British or the German—was to obtain the opportunity and the right to rob, strangle and exploit the whole world. You know that the war settled this question in favor of the British group. And, as a result of this war, all capitalist contradictions have become immeasurably more acute. At a single stroke the war relegated about 250,000,000 of the world's inhabitants to what is equivalent to colonial status, viz., Russia, whose population can be taken at about 130,000,000, and Austria-Hungary, Germany and Bulgaria, with a total population of not less than 120,000,000. That means 250,000,000 people living in countries, of which some, like Germany, are among the most advanced, most enlightened, most cultured, and on a level with modern technical progress. By means of the Treaty of Versailles, the war imposed such terms upon these countries that advanced peoples have been reduced to a state of colonial dependence, poverty, starvation, ruin, and loss of rights: this treaty binds them for many generations, placing them in conditions that no civilised nation has ever lived in. The following is the post-war picture of the world: at least 1, 250 million people are at once brought under the colonial yoke, exploited by a brutal capitalism, which once boasted of its love for peace, and ha   some right to do so some fifty years ago, when the world was not yet partitioned, the monopolies did not as yet rule, and capitalism could still develop in a relatively peaceful way, without tremendous military conflicts.

Today, after this "peaceful" period, we see a monstrous intensification of oppression, the reversion to a colonial and military oppression that is far worse than before. The Treaty of Versailles has placed Germany and the other defeated countries in a position that makes their economic existence physically impossible, deprives them of all rights, and humiliates them.

How many nations are the beneficiaries? To answer this question we must recall that the population of the United States—the only full beneficiary from the war, a country which, from a heavy debtor, has become a general creditor—is no more than 100,000,000. The population of Japan—which gained a great deal by keeping out of the European-American conflict and by seizing the enormous Asian continent—is 50,000,000. The population of Britain, which next to the above-mentioned countries gained most, is about 50,000,000. If we add the neutral countries with their very small populations, countries which were enriched by the war, we shall get, in round figures, some 250,000,000 people.

Thus you get the broad outlines of the picture of the world as it appeared after the imperialist war. In the oppressed colonies—countries which are being dismembered, such as Persia, Turkey and China, and in countries that were defeated and have been relegated to the position of colonies—there are 1,250 million inhabitants. Not more than 250,000,000 inhabit countries that have retained their old positions, but have become economically dependent upon America, and all of which, during the war, were militarily dependent, once the war involved the whole world and did not permit a single state to remain really neutral. And, finally, we have not more than 250,000 000 inhabitants in countries whose top stratum, the capitalists alone, benefited from the partition of the world. We thus get a total of about 1,750 million comprising the entire population of the world. I would like to remind you of this picture of the world, for all the basic contradictions of capitalism, of imperialism, which are leading up to revolution, all the basic contradictions in the working-class movement that have led up to the furious struggle against the Second International, facts our chairman has referred to, are all connected with this partitioning of the world's population.

Of course, these figures give the economic picture of the world only approximately, in broad outline. And, comrades, it is natural that, with the population of the world divided in this way, exploitation by finance capital, the capitalist monopolies, has increased many times over.

Not only have the colonial and the defeated countries been reduced to a state of dependence; within each victor state the contradictions have grown more acute; all the capitalist contradictions have become aggravated. I shall illustrate this briefly with a few examples.

Let us take the national debts. We know that the debts of the principal European states increased no less than *sevenfold* in the period between 1914 and 1920. I shall quote another economic source, one of particular significance—Keynes, the British diplomat and author of *The Economic Consequenices of the Peace*, who, on instructions from his government, took part in the Versailles peace negotiations, observed them on the spot from thc purely bourgeois point of view, studied the subject in detail, step by step, and took part in the conferences as an economist. He has arrived at conclusions which are more weighty, more striking and more instructive than any a Communist revolutionary could draw, because they are the conclusions of a well-known bourgeois and implacable enemy of Bolshevism, which he, like the British philistine he is, imagines as something monstrous, ferocious, and bestial. Keynes has reached the conclusion that after the Peace of Versailles, Europe and the whole world are heading for bankruptcy. He has resigned, and thrown his book in the government's face with the words: "What you are doing is madness". I shall quote his figures, which can be summed up as follows.

What are the debtor-creditor relations that have developed between the principal powers? I shall convert pounds sterling into gold rubles, at a rate of ten gold rubles to one pound. Here is what we get: the United States has assets amounting to 19,000 million, its liabilities are nil. Before the war it was in Britain's debt. In his report on April 14, 1920, to the last congress of the Communist Party of Germany, Comrade Levi very correctly pointed out that there are now only two powers in the world that can act independently, viz., Britain and America. America alone is absolutely independent financially. Before the war she was a debtor; she is now a creditor only. All the other powers in the world are debtors. Britain has been reduced to a position in which her assets total 17,000 million, and her liabilities 8,000 million. She is already half-way to becoming a debtor nation. Moreover, her assets include about 6,000 million owed to her by Russia. Included in the debt are military supplies received by Russia during the war. When Krasin, as representative of the Russian Soviet Government, recently had occasion to discuss with Lloyd George the subject of debt agreements, he made it plain to the scientists and politicians, to the British Government's leaders, that they were labouring under a strange delusion if they were counting on getting these debts repaid. The British diplomat Keynes has already laid this delusion bare.

Of course, it is not only or even not at all a question of the Russian revolutionary government having no wish to pay the debts. No government would pay, because these debts are usurious interest on a sum that has been paid twenty times over, and the selfsame bourgeois Keynes, who does not in the least sympathise with the Russian revolutionary movement, says: "It is clear that these debts cannot be taken into account."

In regard to France, Keynes quotes the following figures: her assets amount to 3,500 million, and her liabilities to 10,500 million! And this is a country which the French themselves called the world's money-lender, because her "savings" were enormous; the proceeds of colonial and financial pillage—a gigantic capital—enabled her to grant thousands upon thousands of millions in loans, particularly to Russia. These loans brought in an enormous revenue. Notwithstanding this and notwithstanding victory, France has been reduced to debtor status.

A bourgeois American source, quoted by Comrade Braun, a Communist, in his book *Who Must Pay the War Debts?* (Leipzig, 1920), estimates the ratio of debts to national wealth as follows: in the victor countries, Britain and France, the ratio of debts to aggregate national wealth is over 50 per cent; in Italy the percentage is between 60 and 70, and in Russia 90. As you know, however, these debts do not disturb us, because we followed Keynes's excellent advice just a little before his book appeared—we annulled all our debts. (*Stormy applause.*)

In this, however, Keynes reveals the usual crankiness of the philistine: while advising that all debts should be annulled, he goes on to say that, of course, France only stands to gain by it, that, of course, Britain will not lose very much, as nothing can be got out of Russia in any case; America will lose a fair amount, but Keynes counts on American "generosity"! On this point our views differ from those of Keynes and other petty-bourgeois pacifists. We think that to get the debts annulled they will have to wait for something else to happen, and will have to try working in a direction other than counting on the "generosity" of the capitalists.

These few figures go to show that the imperialist war has created an impossible situation for the victor powers as well. This is further shown by the enormous disparity between wages and price rises. On March 8 of this year, the Supreme Economic Council, an institution charged with protecting the bourgeois system throughout the world from the mounting revolution, adopted a resolution which ended with an appeal for order, industry and thrift, provided, of course, the workers remain the slaves of capital. This Supreme Economic Council, organ of the Entente and of the capitalists of the whole world, presented the following summary.

In the United States of America food prices have risen, on the average, by 120 per cent, whereas wages have increased only by 100 per cent. In Britain, food prices have gone up by 170 per cent, and wages 130 per cent; in France, food prices—300 per cent,. and wages 200 per cent; in Japan—food prices 130 per cent, and wages 60 per cent (I have analysed Comrade Braun's figures in his pamphlet and those of the Supreme Economic Council as published in *The Times* of March 10, 1920).

In such circumstances, the workers' mounting resentment, the growth of a revolutionary temper and ideas, and the increase in spontaneous mass strikes are obviously inevitable, since the position of the workers is becoming intolerable. The workers' own experience is convincing them that the capitalists have become prodigiously enriched by the war and are placing the burden of war costs and debts upon the workers' shoulders. We recently learnt by cable that America wants to deport another 500 Communists to Russia so as to get rid of "dangerous agitators".

Even if America deports to our country, not 500 but 500,000 Russian, American, Japanese and French "agitators" that will make no difference, because there will still be the disparity between prices and wages, which they can do nothing about. The reason why they can do nothing about it is because private property is most strictly safeguarded, is "sacred" there. That should not be forgotten, because it is only in Russia that the exploiters' private property has been abolished. The capitalists can do nothing about the gap between prices and wages, and the workers cannot live on their previous wages. The old methods are useless against this calamity. Nothing can be achieved by isolated strikes, the parliamentary struggle, or the vote, because "private property is sacred", and the capitalists have accumulated such debts that the whole world is in bondage to a handful of men. Meanwhile the workers' living conditions are becoming more and more unbearable. There is no other way out but to abolish the exploiters' "private property".

In his pamphlet *Britain and the World Revolution*, valuable extracts from which were published by our *Bulletin of the People's Commissariat of Foreign Affairs* of February 1920, Comrade Lapinsky points out that in Britain coal export prices have doubled as against those anticipated by official industrial circles.

In Lancashire things have gone so far that shares are at a premium of 400 per cent. Bank profits are at least 40-50 per cent. It should, moreover, be noted that, in determining bank profits, all bank officials are able to conceal the lion's share of profits by calling them, not profits but bonuses, commissions, etc. So here, too, indisputable economic facts prove that the wealth of a tiny handful of people has grown prodigiously and that their luxury beggars description, while the poverty of the working class is steadily growing. We must particularly note the further circumstance brought out very clearly by Comrade Levi in the report I have just referred to, namely, the change in the value of money. Money has everywhere depreciated as a result of the debts, the issue of paper currency, etc. The same bourgeois source I have already mentioned, namely, the statement of the Supreme Economic Council of March 8, 1920, has calculated that in Britain the depreciation in the value of currency as against the dollar is approximately one-third, in France and Italy two-thirds, and in Germany as much as 96 per cent.

This fact shows that the "mechanism" of the world capitalist economy is falling apart. The trade relations on which the acquisition of raw materials and the sale of commodities hinge under capitalism cannot go on; they cannot continue to be based on the subordination of a number of countries to a single country—the reason being the change in the value of money. No wealthy country can exist or trade unless it sells its goods and obtains raw materials.

Thus we have a situation in which America, a wealthy country that all countries are subordinate to, cannot buy or sell. And the selfsame Keynes who went through the entire gamut of the Versailles negotiations has been compelled to acknowledge this impossibility despite his unyielding determination to defend capitalism, and all his hatred of Bolshevism. Incidentally, I do not think any communist manifesto, or one that is revolutionary in general, could compare in forcefulness with those pages in Keynes's book which depict Wilson and "Wilsonism" in action. Wilson was the idol of philistines and pacifists like Keynes and a number of heroes of the Second International (and even of the "Two-and-a-Half" International[2]), who exalted the "Fourteen Points" and even wrote "learned" books about the "roots " of Wilson 's policy; they hoped that Wilson would save "social peace", reconcile

[2] This international organization was being set up at the time by the Centrist socialist parties and groups which had left the Second International under pressure from the revolutionary masses. The International Union of the Socialist Parties, as the new organization was officially called was formed at a conference in Vienna in February 1921 and; was also known as the Two-and-a-Half or Vienna International. Professing opposition to the Second International, the leaders of the Two-and-a-Half International actually pursued the same opportunist and splitting policy on the most important questions of the proletarian movement and tried to make the new organization a counter-balance to the growing innuence of the Communists among the workers. Lenin wrote, "The gentlemen of the Two-and-a-Half International pose as revolutionaries; but in every serious situation they prove to be counter-revolutionaries because they shrink from the violent destruction of the old state machine; they have no faith in the forces of the working class"

In May 1923 the Second International and the Two-and-a-Half International united to form the so-called Labor and Socialist International;—Editor.

exploiters and exploited, and bring about social reforms. Keynes showed vividly how Wilson was made a fool of, and all these illusions were shattered at the first impact with the practical, mercantile and huckster policy of capital as personified by Clemenceau and Lloyd George. The masses of the workers now see more clearly than ever, from their own experience—and the learned pedants could see it just by reading Keynes's book—that the "roots" of Wilson's policy lay in sanctimonious piffle, petty-bourgeois phrase-mongering, and an utter inability to understand the class struggle.

In consequence of all this, two conditions, two fundamental situations, have inevitably and naturally emerged. On the one hand, the impoverishment of the masses has grown incredibly, primarily among 1,250 million people, i.e., 70 per cent of the world's population. These are the colonial and dependent countries whose inhabitants possess no legal rights, countries "mandated" to the brigands of finance. Besides, the enslavement of the defeated countries has been sanctioned by the Treaty of Versailles and by existing secret treaties regarding Russia, whose validity, it is true, is sometimes about as real as that of the scraps of paper stating that we owe so many thousands of millions. For the first time in world history, we see robbery, slavery, dependence, poverty and starvation imposed upon 1,250 million people by a legal act.

On the other hand, the workers in each of the creditor countries have found themselves in conditions that are intolerable. The war has led to an unprecedented aggravation of all capitalist contradictions, this being the origin of the intense revolutionary ferment that is ever growing. During the war people were put under military discipline, hurled into the ranks of death, or threatened with immediate wartime punishment. Because of the war conditions people could not see the economic realities. Writers, poets, the clergy, the whole press were engaged in nothing but glorifying the war. Now that the war has ended, the exposures have begun: German imperialism with its Peace of Brest-Litovsk has been laid bare; the Treaty of Versailles, which was to have been a victory for imperialism but proved its defeat, has been exposed. Incidentally, the example of Keynes shows that in Europe and America tens and hundreds of thousands of petty-bourgeois, intellectuals, and simply more or less literate and educated people, have had to follow the road taken by Keynes, who resigned and threw in the face of the government a book exposing it. Keynes has shown what is taking place and will take place in the minds of thousands and hundreds of thousands of people when they realize that all the speeches about a "war for liberty", etc., were sheer deception, and that as a result only a handful of people were enriched, while the others were ruined and reduced to slavery. Is it not a fact that the bourgeois Keynes declares that, to survive and save the British economy, the British must secure the resumption of free commercial intercourse between Germany and Russia? How can this be achieved? By cancelling all debts, as Keynes proposes. This is an idea that has been arrived at not only by Keynes, the learned economist; millions of people are or will be getting the same idea. And millions of people hear bourgeois economists declare that there is no way out except annulling the debts; therefore "damn the Bolsheviks" (who have annulled the debts), and let us appeal to America's "generosity"! I think that, on behalf of the Congress of the Communist International, we should send a message of thanks to these economists, who have been agitating for Bolshevism.

If, on the one hand, the economic position of the masses has become intolerable, and, on the other hand, the disintegration described by Keynes has set in and is growing among the negligible minority of all-powerful victor countries, then we are in the presence of the maturing of the two conditions for the world revolution.

We now have before us a somewhat more complete picture of the whole world. We know what dependence upon a handful of rich men means to 1,250 million people who have been placed in intolerable conditions of existence. On the other hand, when the peoples were presented with the League of Nations Covenant, declaring that the League had put an end to war and would henceforth not permit anyone to break the peace, and when this Covenant, the last hope of working people all over the world, came into force, it proved to be a victory of the first order for us. Before it came into force, people used to say that it was impossible not to impose special conditions on a country like Germany, but when the Covenant was drawn up, everything would come out all right. Yet, when the Covenant was published, the bitterest opponents of Bolshevism were obliged to repudiate it. When the Covenant came into operation, it appeared that a small group of the richest countries, the "Big Four"—in the persons of Clemenceau, Lloyd George, Orlando and Wilson—had been put on the job of creating the new relations! When the machinery of the Covenant was put into operation, this led to a complete breakdown.

We saw this in the case of the wars against Russia. Weak, ruined and crushed, Russia, a most backward country, fought against all the nations, against a league of the rich and powerful states that dominate the world, and emerged victorious. We could not put up a force that was anything like the equal of theirs, and yet we proved the victors. Why was that? Because there was not a jot of unity among them, because each power worked against the other. France wanted Russia to pay her debts and become a formidable force against Germany; Britain wanted to partition Russia, and attempted to seize the Baku oilfields and conclude a treaty with the border states of Russia. Among the official British documents there is a Paper which scrupulously enumerates all the states (fourteen in all) which some six months ago, in December 1919, pledged themselves to take Moscow and Petrograd. Britain based her policy on these states, to whom she granted loans running into millions. All these calculations have now misfired, and all the loans are unrecoverable.

Such is the situation created by the League of Nations. Every day of this Covenant's existence provides the best propaganda for Bolshevism, since the most powerful adherents of the capitalist "order" are revealing that, on every question, they put spokes in one another's wheels. Furious wrangling over the partitioning of Turkey, Persia, Mesopotamia and China is going on between Japan, Britain, America and France. The bourgeois press in these countries is full of the bitterest attacks and the angriest statements against their "colleagues" for trying to snatch the booty from under their noses. We see complete discord at the top, among this handful, this very small number of extremely rich countries. There are 1,250 million people who find it impossible to live in the conditions of servitude which "advanced" and civilised capitalism wishes to impose on them: after all, these represent 70 per cent of the world's population. This handful of the richest states—Britain, America and Japan (though Japan was able to plunder the Eastern, the Asian countries, she cannot constitute an independent financial and military force without support from another country)—these two or three countries are unable to organise economic relations, and are directing their policies toward disrupting policies of their colleagues and partners in the League of Nations. Hence the world crisis; it is these economic roots of the crisis that provide the chief reason of the brilliant successes the Communist International is achieving.

Comrades, we have now come to the question of the revolutionary crisis as the basis of our revolutionary action. And here we must first of all note two widespread errors. On the one hand, bourgeois economists depict this crisis simply as "unrest", to use the elegant expression of the British. On the other hand, revolutionaries sometimes try to prove that the crisis is absolutely insoluble.

This is a mistake. There is no such thing as an absolutely hopeless situation. The bourgeoisie are behaving like barefaced plunderers who have lost their heads; they are committing folly after folly, thus aggravating the situation and hastening their doom. All that is true. But nobody can "prove" that it is absolutely impossible for them to pacify a minority of the exploited with some petty concessions, and suppress some movement or uprising of some section of the oppressed and exploited. To try to "prove" in advance that there is "absolutely" no way out of the situation would be sheer pedantry, or playing with concepts and catchwords. Practice alone can serve as real "proof" in this and similar questions. All over the world, the bourgeois system is experiencing a tremendous revolutionary crisis. The revolutionary parties must now "prove" in practice that they have sufficient understanding and organization, contact with the exploited masses, and determination and skill to utilise this crisis for a successful, a victorious revolution.

It is mainly to prepare this "proof" that we have gathered at this Congress of the Communist International.

To illustrate to what extent opportunism still prevails among parties that wish to affiliate to the Third International, and how far the work of some parties is removed from preparing the revolutionary class to utilise the revolution ary crisis, I shall quote the leader of the British Independent Labour Party, Ramsay MacDonald. In his book, *Parliament and Revolution*, which deals with the basic problems that are now engaging our attention, MacDonald describes the state of affairs in what is something like a bourgeois pacifist spirit. He admits that there is a revolutionary crisis and that revolutionary sentiments are growing, that the sympathies of the workers are with the Soviets and the dictatorship of the proletariat (note that this refers to Britain) and that the dictatorship of the proletariat is better than the present dictatorship of the British bourgeoisie.

But MacDonald remains a thorough-paced bourgeois pacifist and compromiser, a petty bourgeois who dreams of a government that stands above classes. Like all bourgeois liars, sophists and pedants, MacDonald recognizes the class struggle merely as a "descriptive fact". He ignores the experience of Kerensky, the Mensheviks and the Socialist Revolutionaries of Russia, the similar experience of Hungary, Germany, etc., in regard to creating a "democratic" government allegedly standing above classes. MacDonald lulls his party and those workers who have the misfortune to regard this bourgeois as a socialist, this philistine as a leader, with the words: "We know that all this [i.e., the revolutionary crisis, the revolutionary ferment] will pass . . . settle down." The war, he says, inevitably provoked the crisis, but after the war it will all "settle down", even if not at once!

That is what has been written by a man who is leader of a party that wants to affiliate to the Third International. This is a revelation—the more valuable for its rare outspokenness—of what is no less frequently to be seen in the top ranks of the French Socialist Party and the German Independent Social-Democratic Party, namely, not merely an inability, but also an unwillingness to take advantage, in a revolutionary sense, of the revolutionary crisis, or, in other words, both an inability and an unwillingness to really prepare the party and the class in revolutionary fashion for the dictatorship of the proletariat.

That is the main evil in very many parties which are now leaving the Second International. This is precisely why, in the theses I have submitted to the present Congress, I have dwelt most of all on the tasks connected with *preparations* for the dictatorship of the proletariat, and have given as concrete and exact a definition of them as possible.

Here is another example. A new book against Bolshevism was recently published. An unusually large number of books of this, kind are now coming out in Europe and America; the more anti-Bolshevik books are brought out, the more strong ly and rapidly mass sympathy for Bolshevism grows. I am referring to Otto Bauer's *Bolshevism or Social-Democracy?* This book clearly demonstrates to the Germans the essence of Menshevism, whose shameful role in the Russian revolution is understood well enough by the workers of all countries. Otto Bauer has produced a thoroughgoing Menshevik pamphlet, although he has concealed his own sympathy with Menshevism. In Europe and America, however, more precise information should now be disseminated about what Menshevism actually is, for it is a generic term for all allegedly socialist, Social-Democratic and other trends that are hostile to Bolshevism. It would be dull writing if we Russians were to explain to Europeans what Menshevism is. Otto Bauer has shown that in his book, and we thank in advance the bourgeois and opportunist publishers who will publish it and translate it into various languages. Bauer's book will be a useful if peculiar supplement to the textbooks on communism. Take any paragraph, any argument in Otto Bauer's book and indicate the Menshevism in it, where the roots lie of views that lead up to the actions of the traitors to socialism, of the friends of Kerensky, Scheidemann, etc.—this is a question that could be very usefully and successfully set in "examinations" designed to test whether communism has been properly assimilated. If you cannot answer this question, you are not yet a Communist, and should not join the Communist Party. (*Applause.*)

Otto Bauer has excellently expressed in a single sentence the essence of the views of world opportunism; for this, if we could do as we please in Vienna, we would put up a monument to him in his lifetime. The use of force in the class struggle in modern democracies, Otto Bauer says, would be "violence exercised against the social factors of force".

You may think that this sounds queer and unintelligible. It is an example of what Marxism has been reduced to, of the kind of banality and defence of the exploiters to which the most revolutionary theory can be reduced. A German variety of philistinism is required, and you get the "theory" that the "social factors of force" are: number; the degree of organization; the place held in the process of production and distribution; activity and education. If a rural agricultural labourer or an urban working man practices revolutionary violence against a landowner or a capitalist, that is no dictatorship of the proletarlat, no violence against the exploiters and the oppressors of the people. Oh, no! This is "violence against the social factors of force".

Perhaps my example sounds something like a jest. However, such is the nature of present-day opportunism that its struggle against Bolshevism becomes a jest. The task of involving the working class, all its thinking elements, in the struggle between international Menshevism (the MacDonalds, Otto Bauers and Co.) and Bolshevism is highly useful and very urgent to Europe and America.

Here we must ask: how is the persistence of such trends in Europe to be explained? Why is this opportunism stronger in Western Europe than in our country? It is because the culture of the advanced countries has been, and still is, the result of their being able to live at the expense of a thousand million oppressed people. It is because the capitalists of these countries obtain a great deal more in this way than they could obtain as profits by plundering the workers in their own countries.

Before the war, it was calculated that the three richest countries—Britain, France and Germany—got between eight and ten thousand million francs a year from the export of capital alone, apart from other sources.

It goes without saying that, out of this tidy sum, at least five hundred millions can be spent as a sop to the labour leaders and the labor aristocracy, i.e., on all sorts of bribes. The whole thing boils down to nothing but bribery. It is done in a thousand different ways: by increasing cultural facilities in the largest centres, by creating educational institutions, and by providing co-operative, trade union and parliamentary leaders with thousands of cushy jobs. This is done wherever present-day civilised capitalist relations exist. It is these thousands of millions in super-profits that form the economic basis of opportunism in the working-class movement. In America, Britain and France we see a far greater persistence of the opportunist leaders, of the upper crust of the working class, the labor aristocracy; they offer stronger resistance to the Communist movement. That is why we must be prepared

to find it harder for the European and American workers'
parties to get rid of this disease than was the case in our country. We know that enormous successes have been achieved in
the treatment of this disease since the Third International
was formed, but we have not yet finished the job; the purg-
ing of the workers' parties, the revolutionary parties of the
proletariat all over the world, of bourgeois influences, of the
opportunists in their ranks, is very far from complete.

I shall not dwell on the concrete manner in which we must
do that; that is dealt with in my published theses. My task
consists in indicating the deep economic roots of this phenom-
enon. The disease is a protracted one; the cure takes longer
than the optimists hoped it-would. Opportunism is our principal enemy. Opportunism in the upper ranks of the working-class movement is bourgeois socialism, not proletarian
socialism. It has been shown in practice that working-class
activists who follow the opportunist trend are better defenders of the bourgeoisie than the bourgeois themselves. Without
their leadership of the workers, the bourgeoisie could not remain in power. This has been proved, not only by the history of
the Kerensky regime in Russia; it has also been proved by the
democratic republic in Germany under its Social-Democratic
government, as well as by Albert Thomas's attitude towards
his bourgeois government. It has been proved by similar experience in Britain and the United States. This is where our
principal enemy is, an enemy we must overcome. We must
leave this Congress firmly resolved to carry on this struggle
to the very end, in all parties. That is our main task.

Compared with this task, the rectification of the errors
of the "Left" trend in communism will be an easy one. In a
number of countries anti-parliamentarianism is to be seen,
which has not been so much introduced by people of petty-
bourgeois origin as fostered by certain advanced contingents

of the proletariat out of hatred for the old parliamentarianism, out of a legitimate, proper and necessary hatred for the conduct of members of parliament in Britain, France, Italy, in all lands. Directives must be issued by the Communist International and the comrades must be made more familiar with the experience of Russia, with the significance of a genuinely proletarian political party. Our work will consist in accomplishing this task. The fight against these errors in the proletarian movement, against these shortcomings, will be a thousand times easier than fighting against those bourgeois who, in the guise of reformists, belong to the old parties of the Second International and conduct the whole of their work in a bourgeois, not proletarian, spirit.

Comrades, in conclusion I shall deal with one other aspect of the subject. Our comrade, the chairman, has said that our Congress merits the title of a World Congress. I think he is right, particularly because we have here quite a number of representatives of the revolutionary movement in the colonial and backward countries. This is only a small beginning, but the important thing is that a beginning has been made. At this Congress we see taking place a union between revolutionary proletarians of the capitalist, advanced countries, and the revolutionary masses of those countries where there is no or hardly any proletariat, i.e., the oppressed masses of colonial, Eastern countries. It is on ourselves that the consolidation of unity depends, and I am sure we shall achieve it. World imperialism shall fall when the revolutionary onslaught of the exploited and oppressed workers in each country, overcoming resistance from petty-bourgeois elements and the influence of the small upper crust of labor aristocrats, merges with the revolutionary onslaught of hundreds of millions of people who have hitherto stood beyond the pale of history, and have been regarded merely as the object of history.

The imperialist war has helped the revolution: from the colonies, the backward countries, and the isolation they lived in, the bourgeoisie levied soldiers for this imperialist war. The British bourgeoisie impressed on the soldiers from India that it was the duty of the Indian peasants to defend Great Britain against Germany; the French bourgeoisie impressed on soldiers from the French colonies that it was their duty to defend France. They taught them the use of arms, a very useful thing, for which we might express our deep gratitude to the bourgeoisie—express our gratitude on behalf of all the Russian workers and peasants, and particularly on behalf of all the Russian Red Army. The imperialist war has drawn the dependent peoples into world history. And one of the most important tasks now confronting us is to consider how the foundation-stone of the organization of the Soviet movement Can be laid in the non-capitalist countries. Soviets are possible there; they will not be workers' Soviets, but peasants' Soviets, or Soviets of working people.

Much work will have to be done; errors will be inevitable; many difficulties will be encountered along this road. It is the fundamental task of the Second Congress to elaborate or indicate the practical principles that will enable the work, till now carried on in an unorganized fashion among hundreds of millions of people, to be carried on in an organized, coherent and systematic fashion.

Now, a year or a little more after the First Congress of the Communist International, we have emerged victors over the Second International; it is not only among the workers of the civilised countries that the ideas of the Soviets have spread; it is not only to them that they have become known and intelligible. The workers of all lands are ridiculing the wiseacres, not a few of whom call themselves socialists and argue in a learned or almost learned manner about the Soviet "system", as the German systematists are fond of calling it, or the Soviet "idea" as the British Guild Socialists[3] call it. Not infrequently, these arguments about the Soviet "system" or "idea" becloud the workers' eyes and their minds. However, the workers are brushing this pedantic rubbish aside and are taking up the weapon provided by the Soviets. A recognition of the role and significance of the Soviets has now also spread to the lands of the East.

The groundwork has been laid for the Soviet movement all over the East, all over Asia, among all the colonial peoples.

The proposition that the exploited must rise up against the exploiters and establish their Soviets is not a very complex one. After our experience, after two and a half years of the existence of the Soviet Republic in Russia, and after the First Congress of the Third International, this idea is becoming accessible to hundreds of millions of people oppressed by the exploiters all over the world. We in Russia are often obliged to compromise, to bide our time, since we are weaker than the international imperialists, yet we know that we are defending the interests of this mass of a thousand and a quarter million people. For the time being, we are hampered by barriers, prejudices and ignorance which are receding into the past with every passing hour; but we are more and more becoming representatives and genuine defenders of this 70 per cent of the world's population, this mass of working and

---

[3] Guild socialists—a reformist trend in the British trade unions which arose before the First World War. They denied the class character of the state and sowed illusions among the workers that it was possible to get rid of exploitation without the class struggle, by establishing, on the basis of the existing trade unions, special associations of producers, so-called guilds whose federation was to take over industrial management. In this way the guild socialists hoped to build socialism.

After the October Socialist Revolution the Guild socialists stepped up their propaganda, contraposing the "theory" of guild socialism to the ideas of the class struggle and the dictatorship of the proletariat. In the 1920s guild socialism lost all its influence on the British workers;—*Editor.*

exploited people. It is with pride that we can say: at the First Congress we were in fact merely propagandists; we were only spreading the fundamental ideas among tbe world's proletariat; we only issued the call for struggle; we were merely asking where the people were who were capable of taking this path. Today the advanced proletariat is everywhere with us. A proletarian army exists everywhere, although sometimes it is poorly organized and needs reorganizing. If our comrades in all lands help us now to organise a united army, no shortcomings will prevent us from accomplishing our task. That task is the world proletarian revolution, the creation of a world Soviet republic. (*Prolonged applause.*)

2

**Speech On The Role Of The Communist Party
July 23**

Comrades, I would like to make a few remarks concerning the speeches of Comrades Tanner and McLaine. Tanner says that he stands for the dictatorship of the proletariat, but he does not see the dictatorship of the proletariat quite in the way we do. He says that by the dictatorship of the proletariat we actually mean the dictatorship of the organized and class-conscious minority of the proletariat.

True enough, in the era of capitalism, when the masses of the workers are subjected to constant exploitation and cannot develop their human capacities, the most characteristic feature of working-class political parties is that they can involve only a minority of their class. A political party can comprise only a minority of a class, in the same way as the really class-conscious workers in any capitalist society constitute only a minority of all workers. We are therefore obliged to recognize

that it is only this class-conscious minority that can direct
and lead the broad masses of the workers. And if Comrade
Tanner says that he is opposed to parties, but at the same
time is in favor of a minority that represents the best organized and most revolutionary workers showing the way to the
entire proletariat, then I say that there is really no difference
between us. What is this organized minority? If this minority
is really class-conscious, if it is able to lead the masses, if it is
able to reply to every question that appears on the order of the
day, then it is a party in reality. But if comrades like Tanner, to whom we pay special heed as representatives of a mass
movement—which cannot, without a certain exaggeration, be
said of the representatives of the British Socialist Party—if
these comrades are in favor of there being a minority that will
fight resolutely for the dictatorship of the proletariat and will
educate the masses of the workers along these lines, then this
minority is in reality nothing but a party. Comrade Tanner
says that this minority should organise and lead the entire
mass of workers. If Comrade Tanner and the other comrades
of the Shop Stewards' group and the Industrial Workers of
the World accept this—and we see from the daily talks we
have had with them that they do accept it—if they approve
the idea that the class-conscious Communist minority of the
working class leads the proletariat, then they must also agree
that this is exactly the meaning of all our resolutions. In that
case the only difference between us lies in their avoidance of
the word "party" because there exists among the British comrades a certain mistrust of political parties. They can conceive
of political parties only in the image of the parties of Gompers
and Henderson,[4] parties of parliamentary smart dealers and

---

[4]   The reference is to the American Federation of Labor and the British Labour Party.

The American Federation of Labor was formed in 1881, on the guild principle.
In the main it organized the labour aristocracy. The reformist A.F.L. leaders

traitors to the working class. But if, by parliamentarianism, they mean what exists in Britain and America today, then we too are opposed to such parliamentarianism and to such political parties. What we want is new and different parties. We want parties that will be in constant and real contact with the masses and will be able to lead those masses.

I now come to the third question I want to touch upon in connection with Comrade McLaine 's speech. He is in favor of the British Communist Party affiliating to the Labour Party. I have already expressed my opinion on this score in my theses on affiliation to the Third International. In my pamphlet I left the question open. However, after discussing the matter with a number of comrades, I have come to the conclusion that the decision to remain within the Labour Party is the only correct tactic. But here is Comrade Tanner, who declares, "Don't be too dogmatic." I consider his remark quite out of place here. Comrade Ramsay says: "Please let us British Communists decide this question for ourselves." What would the International be like if every little group were to come along and say: "Some of us are in favour of this thing and some are against; leave it to us to decide the matter for ourselves"? What then would be the use of having an International, a congress, and all this discussion? Comrade McLaine spoke only of the role of a political party. But the same applies to the trade unions and to parliamentarianism. It is quite true that a larger section of the finest revolutionaries are against affiliation to the Labour Party because they are opposed to parliamentarianism as a means of struggle. Perhaps it would be best to refer this question to a commission,

denied the principles of socialism and the class struggle, preached "class co-operationn and championed the capitalist system. They followed a splitting policy in the international working-class movement, giving active support to the aggressive policy of the U.S. imperialists. In 1955 the A.F.L. merged with the C.I.O;—Editor.

where it should be discussed and studied, and then decided at this very Congress of the Communist International. We cannot agree that it concerns only the British Communists. We must say, in general, which are the correct tactics.

I will now deal with some of Comrade McLaine's arguments concerning the question of the British Labour Party. We must say frankly that the Party of Communists can join the Labour Party only on condition that it preserves full freedom of criticism and is able to conduct its own policy. This is of supreme importance. When, in this connection Comrade Serrati speaks of class collaboration, I affirm that this will not be class collaboration. When the Italian comrades tolerate, in their party, opportunists like Turati and Co., i.e., bourgeois elements, that is indeed class collaboration. In this instance, however, with regard to the British Labour Party, it is simply a matter of collaboration between the advanced minority of the British workers and their vast majority. Members of the Labour Party are all members of trade unions. It has a very unusual structure, to be found in no other country. It is an organization that embraces four million workers out of the six or seven million organized in trade unions. They are not asked to state what their political opinions are. Let Comrade Serrati prove to me that anyone there will prevent us from exercising our right of criticism. Only by proving that, will you prove Comrade McLaine wrong. The British Socialist Party can quite freely call Henderson a traitor and yet remain in the Labour Party. Here we have collaboration between the vanguard of the working class and the rearguard, the backward workers. This collaboration is so important to the entire movement that we categorically insist on the British Communists serving as a link between the Party, that is, the minority of the working class, and the rest of the workers. If the minority is unable to lead the masses and establish close links with them, then it is not a party, and is worthless in general, even if it calls itself a party or the National Shop Stewards' Committee—as far as I know, the Shop Stewards' Committees in Britain have a National Committee, a central body, and that is a step towards a party. Consequently, until it is refuted that the British Labour Party consists of proletarians, this is co-operation between the vanguard of the working class and the backward workers; if this co-operation is not carried on systematically, the Communist Party will be worthless and there can be no question of the dictatorship of the proletariat at all. If our Italian comrades cannot produce more convincing arguments, we shall have to definitely settle the question later here, on the basis of what we know—and we shall come to the conclusion that affiliation is the correct tactic.

Comrades Tanner and Ramsay tell us that the majority of British Communists will not accept affiliation. But must we always agree with the majority? Not at all. If they have not yet understood which are the correct tactics, then perhaps it would be better to wait. Even the parallel existence for a time of two parties would be better than refusing to reply to the question as to which tactics are correct. Of course, acting on the experience of all Congress delegates and on the arguments that have been brought forward here, you will not insist on passing a resolution here and now, calling for the immediate formation of a single Communist Party in each country. That is impossible. But we can frankly express our opinion, and give directives. We must study in a special commission the question raised by the British delegation and then we shall say: affiliation to the Labour Party is the correct tactic. If the majority is against it, we must organise a separate minority. That will be of educational value. If the masses of the British workers still believe in the old tactics, we shall verify our conclusions at the next congress. We cannot, however, say that this question concerns Britain alone—that would mean copying the worst habits of the Second International. We must express our opinion frankly. If the British Communists do not reach agreement, and if a mass party is not formed, a split is inevitable one way or another.[5]

3

Report Of The Commission On The National and The Colonial Questions

Comrades, I shall confine myself to a brief introduction, after which Comrade Maring, who has been secretary to our commission, will give you a detailed account of the changes we have made in the theses. He will be followed by Comrade Roy, who has formulated the supplementary theses. Our commission have unanimously adopted both the preliminary theses, as amended, and the supplementary theses. We have thus reached complete unanimity on all major issues. I shall now make a few brief remarks.

First, what is the cardinal idea underlying our theses? It is the distinction between oppressed and oppressor nations. Unlike the Second International and bourgeois democracy, we emphasise this distinction. In this age of imperialism, it is particularly important for the proletariat and the Communist

[5]   Issue No. 5 of the Bulletin of The Second Congress of the Communist International gave the concluding sentences of this speech as follows:

"We must express our opinion frankly, whatever it may be. If the British Communists do not reach agreement on the question of the organization of the mass movement, and if a split takes place in this issue, then better a split than rejection of the organization of the mass movement. It is better to rise to definite and sufficiently clear tactics and ideology than to go on remaining in the previous chaos."—*Editor.*

International to establish the concrete economic facts and to proceed from concrete realities, not from abstract postulates, in all colonial and national problems.

The characteristic feature of imperialism consists in the whole world, as we now see, being divided into a large number of oppressed nations and an insignificant number of oppressor nations, the latter possessing colossal wealth and powerful armed forces. The vast majority of the world's population, over a thousand million, perhaps even 1,250 million people, if we take the total population of the world as 1,750 million, in other words, about 70 per cent of the world's population, belong to the oppressed nations, which are either in a state of direct colonial dependence or are semi-colonies, as, for example, Persia, Turkey and China, or else, conquered by some big imperialist power, have become greatly dependent on that power by virtue of peace treaties. This idea of distinction, of dividing the nations into oppressor and oppressed, runs through the theses, not only the first theses published earlier over my signature, but also those submitted by Comrade Roy. The latter were framed chiefly from the standpoint of the situation in India and other big Asian countries oppressed by Britain. Herein lies their great importance to us.

The second basic idea in our theses is that, in the present world situation following the imperialist war, reciprocal relations between peoples and the world political system as a whole are determined by the struggle waged by a small group of imperialist nations against the Soviet movement and the Soviet states headed by Soviet Russia. Unless we bear that in mind, we shall not be able to pose a single national or colonial problem correctly, even if it concerns a most outlying part of the world. The Communist parties, in civilised and backward countries alike, can pose and solve political problems correctly only if they make this postulate their starting-point.

Third, I should like especially to emphasise the question of the bourgeois-democratic movement in backward countries. This is a question that has given rise to certain differences. We have discussed whether it would be right or wrong, in principle and in theory, to state that the Communist International and the Communist parties must support the bourgeois-democratic movement in backward countries. As a result of our discussion, we have arrived at the unanimous decision to speak of the national-revolutionary movement rather than of the "bourgeois-democratic" movement. It is beyond doubt that any national movement can only be a bourgeois-democratic movement, since the overwhelming mass of the population in the backward countries consist of peasants who represent bourgeois-capitalist relationships. It would be utopian to believe that proletarian parties in these backward countries, if indeed they can emerge in them, can pursue communist tactics and a communist policy, without establishing definite relations with the peasant movement and without giving it effective support. However, the objections have been raised that, if we speak of the bourgeois-democratic movement, we shall be obliterating all distinctions between the reformist and the revolutionary movements. Yet that distinction has been very clearly revealed of late in the backward and colonial countries, since the imperialist bourgeoisie is doing everything in its power to implant a reformist movement among the oppressed nations too. There has been a certain *rapprochement* between the bourgeoisie of the exploiting countries and that of the colonies, so that very often— perhaps even in most cases—the bourgeoisie of the oppressed countries, while it does support the national movement, is in full accord with the imperialist bourgeoisie, i.e., joins forces with it against all revolutionary movements and revolutionary classes. This was irrefutably proved in the commission, and we decided that the only correct attitude was to take this distinction into account and, in nearly all cases, substitute the term "national-revolutionary" for the term "bourgeois-democratic". The significance of this change is that we, as Communists, should and will support bourgeois-liberation movements in the colonies only when they are genuinely revolutionary, and when their exponents do not hinder our work of educating and organizing in a revolutionary spirit the peasantry and the masses of the exploited. If these conditions do not exist, the Communists in these countries must combat the reformist bourgeoisie, to whom the heroes of the Second International also belong. Reformist parties already exist in the colonial countries, and in some cases their spokesmen call themselves Social-Democrats and socialists. The distinction I have referred to has been made in all the theses with the result, I think, that our view is now formulated much more precisely.

Next, I would like to make a remark on the subject of peasants' Soviets. The Russian Communists' practical activities in the former tsarist colonies, in such backward countries as Turkestan, etc., have confronted us with the question of how to apply the communist tactics and policy in pre-capitalist conditions. The preponderance of pre-capitalist relationships is still the main determining feature in these countries, so that there can be no question of a purely proletarian movement in them. There is practically no industrial proletariat in these countries. Nevertheless, we have assumed, we must assume, the role of leader even there. Experience has shown us that tremendous difficulties have to be surmounted in these countries. However, the practical results of our work have also shown that despite these difficulties we are in a position to inspire in the masses an urge for independent political thinking and independent political action, even where a proletariat is practically non-existent. This work has been more difficult for us than it will be for comrades in the West-European countries, because in Russia the proletariat is engrossed in the work of state administration. It will really be understood that peasants living in conditions of semi-feudal dependence can easily assimilate and give effect to the idea of Soviet organization. It is also clear that the oppressed masses, those who are exploited, not only by merchant capital but also by the feudalists, and by a state based on feudalism, can apply this weapon, this type of organization, in their conditions too. The idea of Soviet organization is a simple one, and is applicable, not only to proletarian, but also to peasant feudal and semi-feudal relations. Our experience in this respect is not as yet very considerable. However, the debate in the commission, in which several representatives from colonial countries participated, demonstrated convincingly that the Communist International's theses should point out that peasants' Soviets, Soviets of the exploited, are a weapon which can be employed, not only in capitalist countries but also in countries with pre-capitalist relations, and that it is the absolute duty of Communist parties and of elements prepared to form Communist parties, everywhere to conduct propaganda in favor of peasants' Soviets or of working people's Soviets, this to include backward and colonial countries. Wherever conditions permit, they should at once make attempts to set up Soviets the working people.

This opens up a very interesting and very important field for our practical work. So far our joint experience in this respect has not been extensive, but more and more data will gradually accumulate. It is unquestionable that the proletariat of the advanced countries can and should give help to the working masses of the backward countries, and that the backward countries can emerge from their present stage of development when the victorious proletariat of the Soviet Republics extends a helping hand to these masses and is in a position to give them support.

There was quite a lively debate on this question in the commission, not only in connection with the theses I signed, but still more in connection with Comrade Roy's theses, which he will defend here, and certain amendments to which were unanimously adopted.

The question was posed as follows: are we to consider as correct the assertion that the capitalist stage of economic development is inevitable for backward nations now on the road to emancipation and among whom a certain advance towards progress is to be seen since the war? We replied in the negative. If the victorious revolutionary proletariat conducts systematic propaganda among them, and the Soviet governments come to their aid with all the means at their disposal—in that event it will be mistaken to assume that the backward peoples must inevitably go through the capitalist stage of development. Not only should we create independent contingents of fighters and party organizations in the colonies and the backward countries, not only at once launch propaganda for the organization of peasants' Soviets and strive to adapt them to the pre-capitalist conditions, but the Communist International should advance the proposition, with the appropriate theoretical grounding, that with the aid of the proletariat of the advanced countries, backward countries can go over to the Soviet system and, through certain stages of development, to communism, without having to pass through the capitalist stage.

The necessary means for this cannot be indicated in advance. These will be prompted by practical experience. It has, however, been definitely established that the idea of the Soviets is understood by the mass of the working people in even the most remote nations, that the Soviets should be adapted to the conditions of a pre-capitalist social system, and that the Communist parties should immediately begin work in this direction in all parts of the world.

I would also like to emphasise the importance of revolutionary work by the Communist parties, not only in their own, but also in the colonial countries, and particularly among the troops employed by the exploiting nations to keep the colonial peoples in subjection.

Comrade Quelch of the British Socialist Party spoke of this in our commission. He said that the rank-and-file British worker would consider it treasonable to help the enslaved nations in their uprisings against British rule. True, the jingoist and chauvinist-minded labor aristocrats of Britain and America present a very great danger to socialism, and are a bulwark of the Second International. Here we are confronted with the greatest treachery on the part of leaders and workers belonging to this bourgeois International. The colonial question has been discussed in the Second International as well.[6] The Basle Manifesto[7] is quite clear on this point, too. The parties of the Second International have pledged themselves to

[6] The commission on the national and the colonial questions, formed by the Second Congress of the Communist International included representatives of the Communist parties of Russia, Bulgaria, France, Holland, Germany, Hungary, the U.S.A., India, Persia, China, Korea and Britain. The work of the commission was guided by Lenin, whose theses on the national and the colonial questions were discussed at the fourth and fifth sessions of the Congress, and were adopted on July 28;—*Editor.*

[7] The Basle Manifesto was adopted by the Extraordinary International Socialist Congress held in Basle on November 24-25, 1912. It gave a warning against the imminent world imperialist war, whose predatory aims it unmasked, and called upon the workers of all countries to wage a determined fight for peace and "to pit against the might of capitalist imperialism the international solidarity of the proletariat". The Manifesto denounced the expansionist policy of the imperialist countries and urged socialists to fight against all oppression of small nations and manifestations of chauvinism.

revolutionary action, but they have given no sign of genuine revolutionary work or of assistance to the exploited and dependent nations in their revolt against the oppressor nations. This, I think, applies also to most of the parties that have withdrawn from the Second International and wish to join the Third International. We must proclaim this publicly for all to hear, and it is irrefutable. We shall see if any attempt is made to deny it.

All these considerations have formed the basis of our resolutions, which undoubtedly are too lengthy but will nevertheless, I am sure, prove of use and will promote the development and organization of genuine revolutionary work in connection with the national and the colonial questions. And that is our principal task.

4

Speech On The Terms Of Admission
Into The Communist International
July 30[8]

Comrades, Serrati has said that we have not yet invented a sincerometer—meaning by this French neologism an instrument for measuring sincerity. No such instrument has been invented yet. We have no need of one. But we do already have an instrument for defining trends. Comrade Serrati's error, which I shall deal with later, consists in his having failed to use this instrument, which has been known for a long time.

---

[8] The terms of admission into the Communist International were first discussed by a commission appointed by the Congress. The commission included representatives of the Communist parties of Russia, Germany, Bulgaria, the U.S.A., HunRary, Austria, Holland, the Irish I.W.W., the Left wing of the Socialist Party of Switzerland and the French Communist group. In its work the commission proceeded from Lenin's theses "The Terms of Admission into the Communist International". Lenin also worked on the commission. The terms of admission into the Communist International were discussed at three Congress sessions, July 29 and 30, and were adopted on August 6;—*Editor.*

I would like to say only a few words about Comrade Crispien. I am very sorry that he is not present. (*Dittmann*: "He is ill.") I am very sorry to hear it. His speech is a most important document, and expresses explicitly the political line of the Right wing of the Independent Social-Democratic Party. I shall speak, not of personal circumstances or individual cases but only of the ideas clearly expressed in Crispien's speech. I think I shall be able to prove that the entire speech was thoroughly in the Kautskian spirit, and that Comrade Crispien shares the Kautskian views on the dictatorship of the proletariat. Replying to a rejoinder, Crispien said: "Dictatorship is nothing new, it was already mentioned in the Erfurt Programme."[9] The Erfurt Programme says nothing about the dictatorship of the proletariat, and history has proved that this was not due to chance. When in 1902-03, we were drawing up our Party's first programme, we always had before us the example of the Erfurt Programme; Plekhanov, that very Plekhanov who rightly said at the time, "Either Bernstein will bury Social-Democracy, or Social-Democracy will bury Bernstein", laid special emphasis on the fact that the Erfurt Programme's failure to mention the dictatorship of the proletariat was erroneous from the standpoint of theory

[9] Lenin is referring to the German Social-Democratic Party's programme which was adopted at its congress in Erfurt in October 1891. This programme marked an advance over the Gotha Programme of 1875, since it was based on the Marsist thesis that the capitalist mode of production was doomed and would be inevitably replaced by the socialist mode of production; it stressed the need for the working class to wage a political struggle and defined the party's role as leader in that struggle, but it too made serious concessions to opportunism. Engels gave a profound criticism of the draft of the programme in his work "Zur Kritik des sozialdemokratischen Programmentwurfes 1891" (see Marx/Engels, Werke, Dietz Verlag, Berlin, 1963, Bd. 22, S. 225-40). In fact, Engels criticised the opportunism of the entire Second International. However, in working out the final version of the programme, the German Social-Democratic leaders concealed Engels's criticism from the Party rank and file and disregarded his most important remarks. According to Lenin, the fact that the Erfurt Programme made no mention of the dictatorship of the proletafiat was the main defect in the programme, and a cowardly concession to opportunism;—*Editor*.

and, in practice was a cowardly concession to the opportunists. The dictatorship of the proletariat has been in our programme since 1903.

When Comrade Crispien now says that the dictatorship of the proletariat is nothing new, and goes on to say: "We have always stood for the conquest of political power", he is evading the gist of the matter. Conquest of political power is recognized, but not dictatorship. All the socialist literature—not only German, but French and British as well—shows that the leaders of the opportunist parties, for instance, MacDonald in Britain, stand for the conquest of political power. They are, in all conscience, sincere socialists, but they are against the dictatorship of the proletariat! Since we have a good revolutionary party worthy of the name of Communist, it should conduct propaganda for the dictatorship of the proletariat, as distinct from the old conception of the Second International. This has been glossed over and obscured by Comrade Crispien, which is the fundamental error common to all of Kautsky's adherents.

"We are leaders elected by the masses, " Comrade Crispien continues. This is a formal and erroneous point of view, since a struggle of trends was clearly to be seen at the latest Party congress of the German Independents. There is no need to seek for a sincerometer and to wax humorous on the subject, as Comrade Serrati does, in order to establish the simple fact that a struggle of trends must and does exist: one trend is that of the revolutionary workers who have just joined us and are opposed to the labor aristocracy; the other is that of the labor aristocracy, which in all civilised countries is headed by the old leaders. Does Crispien belong to the trend of the old leaders and the labor aristocracy, or to that of the new revolutionary masses of workers, who are opposed to the labor aristocracy? That is a question Comrade Crispien has failed to clarify.

In what kind of tone does Comrade Crispien speak of the split? He has said that the split was a bitter necessity, and deplored the matter at length. That is quite in the Kautskian spirit. Who did they break away from? Was it not from Scheidemann? Of course, it was. Crispien has said: "We have split away." In the first place, this was done too late. Since we are on the subject, that has to be said. Second, the Independents should not deplore this, but should say: "The international working class is still under the sway of the labor aristocracy and the opportunists." Such is the position both in France and in Great Britain. Comrade Crispien does not regard the split like a Communist, but quite in the spirit of Kautsky, who is supposed to have no influence. Then Crispien went on to speak of high wages. The position in Germany, he said, is that the workers are quite well off compared with the workers in Russia or in general, in the East of Europe. A revolution, as he sees it, can be made only if it does not worsen the workers' conditions "too much". Is it permissible, in a Communist Party, to speak in a tone like this, I ask? This is the language of counter-revolution. The standard of living in Russia is undoubtedly lower than in Germany, and when we established the dictatorship, this led to the workers beginning to go more hungry and to their conditions becoming even worse. The workers' victory cannot be achieved without sacrifices, without a temporary deterioration of their conditions. We must tell the workers the very opposite of what Crispien has said. If, in desiring to prepare the workers for the dictatorship, one tells them that their conditions will not be worsened "too much", one is losing sight of the main thing, namely, that it was by helping their "own" bourgeoisie to conquer and strangle the whole world by imperialist methods, with the aim of thereby ensuring better pay for themselves, that the labor aristocracy developed. If the German workers now want to work for the revolution they must make sacrifices, and not be afraid to do so.

In the general and world-historical sense, it is true that in a backward country like China, the coolie cannot bring about a proletarian revolution; however, to tell the workers in the handful of rich countries where life is easier, thanks to imperialist pillage, that they must be afraid of "too great" impoverishment, is counter-revolutionary. It is the reverse that they should be told. The labor aristocracy that is afraid of sacrifices, afraid of "too great" impoverishment during the revolutionary struggle, cannot belong to the Party. Otherwise the dictatorship is impossible, especially in West-European countries.

What does Crispien say about terror and coercion? He has said that these are two different things. Perhaps such a distinction is possible in a manual of sociology, but it cannot be made in political practice, especially in the conditions of Germany. We are forced to resort to coercion and terror against people who behave like the German officers did when they murdered Liebknecht and Rosa Luxemburg, or against people like Stinnes and Krupp, who buy up the press. Of course, there is no need to proclaim in advance that we shall positively resort to terror but if the German officers and the Kappists remain the same as they now are and if Krupp and Stinnes remain the same as they now are, the employment of terror will be inevitable. Not only Kautsky, but Ledebour and Crispien as well, speak of coercion and terror in a wholly counter revolutionary spirit. A party that makes shift with such ideas cannot participate in the dictatorship. That is self evident.

Then there is the agrarian question. Here Crispien has got very worked up and tried to impute a petty-bourgeois spirit to us: to do anything for the small peasant at the expense of the big landowner is alleged to be petty-bourgeois action. He says the landed proprietors should be dispossessed and their land handed over to co-operative associations. This is a pedantic viewpoint. Even in highly developed countries, including Germany, there are a sufficient number of latifundia, landed estates that are cultivated by semi-feudal, not large-scale capitalist, methods. Part of such land may be cut off and turned over to the small peasants, without injury to farming. Large-scale farming can be preserved, and yet the small peasants can be provided with something of considerable importance to them. No thought is given to this, unfortunately, but in practice that has to be done, for otherwise you will fall into error. This has been borne out, for example, in a book by Varga (former People's Commissar for the National Economy in the Hungarian Soviet Republic), who writes that the establishment of the proletarian dictatorship hardly changed anything in the Hungarian countryside, that the day-labourers saw no changes, and the small peasants got nothing. There are large latifundia in Hungary, and a semi-feudal economy is conducted in large areas. Sections of large estates can and must always be found, part of which can be turned over to the small peasants, perhaps not as their property, but on lease, so that even the smallest peasant may get some part of the confiscated estates. Otherwise, the small peasant will see no difference between the old order and the dictatorship of the Soviets. If the proletarian state authority does not act in this way, it will be unable to retain power.

Although Crispien did say: "You cannot deny that we have our revolutionary convictions", I shall reply that I do deny them. I do not say that you would not like to act in revolutionary manner, but I do say that you are unable to reason in a revolutionary fashion. I am willing to wager that if we chose any commission of educated people, and gave them a dozen Kautsky's books and then Crispien's speech, the commission would say: "The whole speech is thoroughly Kautskian, is imbued through and through with Kautsky's views." The entire method of Crispien's argumentation is fundamentally Kautskian, yet Crispien comes along and says, "Kautsky no longer has any influence whatever in our party." No influence, perhaps, on the revolutionary workers who have joined recently. However, it must be accepted as absolutely proved that Kautsky has had and still has an enormous influence on Crispien, on his entire line of thought, all his ideas. This is manifest in his speech. That is why, without inventing any sincerometers, any instruments for measuring sincerity, we can say that Crispien's orientation is not that of the Communist International. In saying this, we are defining the orientation of the entire Communist International.

Comrades Wijnkoop and Munzenberg have expressed dissatisfaction with the fact that we have invited the Independent Socialist Party and are holding talks with its representatives. I think they are wrong. When Kautsky attacks us and brings out books against us, we polemise with him as our class enemy. But when the Independent Social-Democratic Party, which has expanded as a result of an influx of revolutionary workers, comes here for negotiations, we must talk to its representatives, since they are a section of the revolutionary workers. We cannot reach an immediate agreement with the German Independents, or with the French and the British, regarding the International. In every speech he delivers, Comrade Wijnkoop reveals that he shares almost all the errors of Comrade Pannekoek. Wijnkoop has stated that he does not share Pannekoek's views; but his speeches prove the reverse. Herein lies the main error of this "Left" group, but this, in general, is an error of a proletarian movement that is developing. The speeches of Comrades Crispien and Dittmann are imbued with a bourgeois spirit which will not help us prepare for the dictatorship of the proletariat. When Comrades Wijnkoop and Muinzenberg go still further on the subject of the Independent Social-Democratic Party, we are not in agreement with them.

Of course, we have no instrument for measuring sincerity, as Serrati has put it, for testing a man's conscience; we quite agree that the matter is not one of forming an opinion of people, but of appraising a situation. I am sorry to say that although Serrati did speak he said nothing new. His was the sort of speech we used to hear in the Second International as well.

Serrati was wrong in saying: "In France the situation is not revolutionary; in Germany it is revolutionary; in Italy it is revolutionary."

Even if the situation is non-revolutionary, the Second International is in error and carries a heavy responsibility if it is really unwilling to organise revolutionary propaganda and agitation, since, as has been proved by the entire history of the Bolshevik Party, revolutionary propaganda can and should be conducted even in a situation that is not revolutionary. The difference between the socialists and the Communists consists in the former refusing to act in the way we act in any situation, i.e., conduct revolutionary work.

Serrati merely repeats what Crispien has said. We do not mean to say that Turati should be expelled on such and such a date. That question has already been touched upon by the

Executive Committee, and Serrati has said to us: "Not expulsions, but a Party purge." We must simply tell the Italian comrades that it is the line of *L'Ordine Nuovo* members that corresponds to the line of the Communist International, and not that of the present majority of the Socialist Party's leaders and their parliamentary group. They claim that they want to defend the proletariat against the reactionaries. Chernov, the Mensheviks and many others in Russia are also "defending" the proletariat against the reactionaries, but that is not sufficient reason for accepting them into our midst.

That is why we must say to the Italian comrades and all parties that have a Right wing: this reformist tendency has nothing in common with communism.

We ask our Italian comrades to call a congress and have our theses and resolutions submitted to it. I am sure that the Italian workers will want to remain in the Communist International.

<h3 style="text-align:center">5</h3>

Speech On Parliamentarianism
August 2

Comrade Bordiga seems to have wanted to defend the Italian Marxists' point of view here, yet he has failed to reply to any of the arguments advanced by other Marxists in favor of parliamentary action.

Comrade Bordiga has admitted that historical experience is not created artificially. He has just told us that the struggle must be carried into another sphere. Is he not aware that every revolutionary crisis has been attended by a parliamentary crisis? True, he has said that the struggle must be carried into another sphere, into the Soviets. Bordiga, however, has himself admitted that Soviets cannot be created artificially. The example of Russia shows that Soviets can be organized either during a revolution or on the eve of a revolution. Even in the Kerensky period, the Soviets (which were Menshevik Soviets) were organized in such a way that they could not possibly constitute a proletarian government. Parliament is a product of historical development, and we cannot eliminate it until we are strong enough to disperse the bourgeois parliament. It is only as a member of the bourgeois parliament that one can, in the given historical conditions, wage a struggle against bourgeois society and parliamentarianism. The same weapon as the bourgeoisie employs in the struggle must also be used by the proletariat, of course, with entirely different aims. You cannot assert that that is not the case, and if you want to challenge it, you will have thereby to erase the experience of all revolutionary developments in the world.

You have said that the trade unions are also opportunist, that they, too, constitute a danger. On the other hand, however, you have said that an exception must be made in the case of trade unions, because they are workers' organizations. But that is true only up to a certain point. There are very backward elements in the trade unions too: a section of the proletarianised petty bourgeoisie, the backward workers, and the small peasants. All these elements really think that their interests are represented in parliament. This idea must be combated by work within parliament and by citing the facts, so as to show the masses the truth. Theory will have no effect on the backward masses; they need practical experience.

This was to be seen in the case of Russia too. We were obliged to convene the Constituent Assembly even after the victory of the proletariat, so as to prove to the backward proletarians that they had nothing to gain from that Assembly. To bring home the difference between the two, we had to concretely contrapose the Soviets and the Constituent Assembly and to show the Soviets as the only solution.

Comrade Souchy, a revolutionary syndicalist, advocated the same theory, but he had no logic on his side. He said that he was not a Marxist, so everything can be readily understood. But you, Comrade Bordiga, assert that you are a Marxist, so we must expect more logic from you. You must know how parliament can be smashed. If you can do it by an armed uprising in all countries, well and good. You are aware that we in Russia proved our determination to destroy the bourgeois parliament, not only in theory, but in practice as well. You, however, have lost sight of the fact that this is impossible without fairly long preparations, and that in most countries it is as yet impossible to destroy parliament at one stroke. We are obliged to carry on a struggle within parliament for the destruction of parliament. For the conditions determining the political line of all classes in modern society you substitute your revolutionary determination; that is why you forget that to destroy the bourgeois parliament in Russia we were first obliged to convene the Constituent Assembly, even after our victory. You say: "It is a fact that the Russian revolution is a case that is not in accord with conditions in Western Europe", but you have not produced a single weighty argument to prove that to us. We went through a period of bourgeois democracy. We went through it rapidly at a time when we had to agitate for elections to the Constituent Assembly. Later, when the working class was able to seize power, the peasants still believed in the necessity of a bourgeois parliament.

Taking account of these backward elements, we had to proclaim the elections and show the masses, by example and by facts, that the Constituent Assembly, which was elected at a time of dire and universal need, did not express the aspirations and demands of the exploited classes. In this way the conflict between Soviet and bourgeois government became quite clear, not only to us, the vanguard of the working class, but also to the vast majority of the peasantry, to the petty office employees, the petty bourgeoisie, etc. In all capitalist countries there are backward elements in the working class who are convinced that parliament is the true representative of the people and do not see the unscrupulous methods employed there. You say that parliament is an instrument with the aid of which the bourgeoisie deceive the masses. But this argument should be turned against you, and it does turn against your theses. How will you reveal the true character of parliament to the really backward masses, who are deceived by the bourgeoisie? How will you expose the various parliamentary manoeuvres, or the positions of the various parties, if you are not in parliament, if you remain outside parliament? If you are Marxists, you must admit that, in capitalist society, there is a close link between the relations of classes and the relations of parties. How, I repeat, will you show all this if you are not members of parliament, and if you renounce parliamentary action? The history of the Russian revolution has clearly shown that the masses of the working class, the peasantry, and petty office employees could not have been convinced by any arguments, unless their own experience had convinced them.

It has been claimed here that it is a waste of time to participate in the parliamentary struggle. Can one conceive of any other institution in which all classes are as interested as they are in parliament? This cannot be created artificially. If all classes are drawn into the parliamentary struggle, it is because the class interests and conaicts are reflected in parliament. If it were possible everywhere and immediately to bring about, let us say, a decisive general strike so as to overthrow capitalism at a single stroke, the revolution would have already taken place in a number of countries. But we must reckon with the facts, and parliament is a scene of the class struggle. Comrade Bordiga and those who share his views must tell the masses the truth. Germany provides the best example that a Communist group in parliament is possible. That is why you should have frankly said to the masses: "We are too weak to create a party with a strong organization." That would be the truth that ought to be told. But if you confessed your weakness to the masses, they would become your opponents, not your supporters; they would become supporters of parliamentarianism.

If you say: "Fellow workers, we are so weak that we cannot form a party disciplined enough to compel its members of parliament to submit to it", the workers would abandon you, for they would ask themselves: "How can we set up a dictatorship of the proletariat with such weaklings?"

You are very naïve if you think that the intelligentsia, the middle class, and the petty bourgeoisie will turn Communist the day the proletariat is victorious.

If you do not harbour this illusion, you should begin right away to prepare the proletariat to pursue its own line. You will find no exceptions to this rule in any branch of state affairs. On the day following the revolution, you will everywhere find advocates of opportunism who call themselves-Communists, i.e., petty bourgeois who refuse to recognize the discipline of the Communist Party or of the proletarian state. Unless you prepare the workers for the creation of a really disciplined party, which will compel its members to submit to its discipline, you will never prepare for the dictatorship of the proletariat. I think that this accounts for your unwillingness to admit that the repudiation of parliamentary action by a great many of the new Communist parties stems from their weakness. I am convinced that the vast majority of the really revolutionary workers will follow us and speak up against your anti-parliamentary theses.

6

Speech On Affiliation To The British Labour Party[10]
August 6

Comrades, Comrade Gallacher began his speech by expressing regret at our having been compelled to listen here for the hundredth and the thousandth time to sentences that Comrade McLaine and other British comrades have reiterated a thousand times in speeches, newspapers and magazines. I think there is no need for regret. The old International used the method of referring such questions for decision to the individual parties in the countries concerned. That was a grave error. We may not be fully familiar with the conditions in one country or another, but in this case we are dealing with the principles underlying a Communist Party's tactics. That is very important and, in the name of the Third International, we must herewith clearly state the communist point of view.

First of all, I should like to mention a slight inaccuracy on the part of Comrade McLaine, which cannot be agreed to. He called the Labour Party the political organization of the trade union movement, and later repeated the statement when he said that the Labour Party is "the political expression of the workers organized in trade unions". I have met the same view several times in the paper of the British Socialist Party. It is erroneous, and is partly the cause of the opposition, fully justified in some measure, coming from the British revolutionary workers. Indeed, the concepts "political department

---

[10] The question of the Communist Party's affiliation to the Labour Party was dealt with during the discussion on Lenin's theses on the fundamental tasks of the Communist International, at the closing session of the Congress on August 6. Following Lenin's speech the majority (58 votes against 24, with 2 abstentions) approved affiliation. The Labor leaders, however, refused to grant membership to the Communist Party. ;—*Editor*.

of the trade unions" or "political expression" of the trade union movement, are erroneous. Of course, most of the Labour Party's members are workingmen. However, whether or not a party is really a political party of the workers does not depend solely upon a membership of workers but also upon the men that lead it, and the content of its actions and its political tactics. Only this latter determines whether we really have before us a political party of the proletariat. Regarded from this, the only correct, point of view, the Labour Party is a thoroughly bourgeois party, because, although made up of workers, it is led by reactionaries, and the worst kind of reactionaries at that, who act quite in the spirit of the bourgeoisie. It is an organization of the bourgeoisie, which exists to systematically dupe the workers with the aid of the British Noskes and Scheidemanns.

We have also heard another point of view, defended by Comrade Sylvia Pankhurst and Comrade Gallacher, who have voiced their opinion in the matter. What was the substance of the speeches delivered by Gallacher and many of his friends? They have told us that they are insufficiently linked with the masses. But take the instance of the British Socialist Party, they went on. It is still less linked with the masses and it is a very weak party. Comrade Gallacher has told us here how he and his comrades have organized, and done so really splendidly, the revolutionary movement in Glasgow, in Scotland, how in their wartime tactics they manoeuvred skillfully, how they gave able support to the petty-bourgeois pacifists Ramsay MacDonald and Snowden when they came to Glasgow, and used this support to organise a mass movement against the war.

It is our aim to integrate this new and excellent revolutionary movement—represented here by Comrade Gallacher and his friends—into a Communist Party with genuinely communist, i.e., Marxist tactics. That is our task today. On the one hand, the British Socialist Party is too weak and incapable of properly carrying on agitation among the masses; on the other hand, we have the younger revolutionary elements so well represented here by Comrade Gallacher, who, although in touch with the masses, are not a political party, and in this sense are even weaker than the British Socialist Party and are totally unable to organise their political work. Under these circumstances, we must express our frank opinion on the correct tactics. When, in speaking of the British Socialist Party, Comrade Gallacher said that it is "hopelessly reformist", he was undoubtedly exaggerating. But the general tenor and content of all the resolutions we have adopted here show with absolute clarity that we demand a change, in this spirit, in the tactics of the British Socialist Party; the only correct tactics of Gallacher's friends will consist in their joining the Communist Party without delay, so as to modify its tactics in the spirit of the resolutions adopted here. If you have so many supporters that you are able to organise mass meetings in Glasgow, it will not be difficult for you to bring more than ten thousand new members into the Party. The latest Conference of the British Socialist Party, held in London three or four days ago, decided to assume the name of the Communist Party and introduced into its programme a clause providing for participation in parliamentary elections and affiliation to the Labour Party. Ten thousand organized members were represented at the Conference. It will therefore not be at all difficult for the Scottish comrades to bring into this "Communist Party of Great Britain" more than ten thousand revolutionary workers who are better versed in the art of working among the masses, and thus to modify the old tactics of the British Socialist Party in the sense of better agitation and more revolutionary action. In the commission, Comrade Sylvia Pankhurst pointed out several times that Britain needed "Lefts". I, of course, replied that this was absolutely true, but that one must not overdo this "Leftism". Furthermore she said that they were better pioneers, but for the moment were rather noisy. I do not take this in a bad sense, but rather in a good one, namely, that they are better able to carry on revolutionary agitation. We do and should value this. We expressed this in all our resolutions, for we always emphasise that we can consider a party to be a workers' party only when it is really linked up with the masses and fights against the old and quite corrupt leaders, against both the Right-wing chauvinists and those who, like the Right Independents in Germany, take up an intermediate position. We have asserted and reiterated this a dozen times and more in all our resolutions, which means that we demand a transformation of the old party, in the sense of bringing it closer to the masses.

Sylvia Pankhurst also asked: "Is it possible for a Communist Party to join another political party which still belongs to the Second International?" She replied that it was not. It should, however, be borne in mind that the British Labour Party is in a very special position: it is a highly original type of party, or rather, it is not at all a party in the ordinary sense of the word. It is made up of members of all trade unions, and has a membership of about four million, and allows sufficient freedom to all affiliated political parties. It thus includes a vast number of British workers who follow the lead of the worst bourgeois elements, the social-traitors, who are even worse than Scheidemann, Noske and similar people. At the same time, however, the Labour Party has let the British Socialist Party into its ranks, permitting it to have its own press organs, in which members of the selfsame

Labour Party can freely and openly declare that the party leaders are social-traitors. Comrade McLaine has cited quotations from such statements by the British Socialist Party. I, too, can certify that I have seen in *The Call,* organ of the British Socialist Party, statements that the Labour Party leaders are social-patriots and social-traitors. This shows that a party affiliated to the Labour Party is able, not only to severely criticise but openly and specifically to mention the old leaders by name, and call them social-traitors. This is a very original situation: a party which unites enormous masses of workers, so that it might seem a political party, is nevertheless obliged to grant its members complete latitude. Comrade McLaine has told us here that, at the Labour Party Conference, the British Scheidemanns were obliged to openly raise the question of affiliation to the Third International, and that all party branches and sections were obliged to discuss the matter. In such circumstances, it would be a mistake not to join this party.

In a private talk, Comrade Pankhurst said to me: "If we are real revolutionaries and join the Labour Party, these gentlemen will expel us." But that would not be bad at all. Our resolution says that we favour affiliation insofar as the Labour Party permits sufficient freedom of criticism. On that point we are absolutely consistent. Comrade McLaine has emphasised that the conditions now prevailing in Britain are such that, should it so desire, a political party may remain a revolutionary workers' party even if it is connected with a special kind of labour organization of four million members, which is half trade union and half political and is headed by bourgeois leaders. In such circumstances it would be highly erroneous for the best revolutionary elements not to do everything possible to remain in such a party. Let the Thomases and other social-traitors, whom you have called by that name, expel you. That will have an excellent effect upon the mass of the British workers.

The comrades have emphasised that the labour aristocracy is stronger in Britain than in any other country. That is true. After all, the labour aristocracy has existed in Britain, not for decades but for centuries. The British bourgeoisie, which has had far more experience—democratic experience—than that of any other country, has been able to buy workers over and to create among them a sizable stratum, greater than in any other country, but one that is not so great compared with the masses of the workers. This stratum is thoroughly imbued with bourgeois prejudices and pursues a definitely bourgeois reformist policy. In Ireland, for instance, there are two hundred thousand British soldiers who are applying ferocious terror methods to suppress the Irish. The British Socialists are not conducting any revolutionary propaganda among these soldiers, though our resolutions clearly state that we can accept into the Communist International only those British parties that conduct genuinely revolutionary propaganda among the British workers and soldiers. I emphasise that we have heard no objections to this either here or in the commissions.

Comrades Gallacher and Sylvia Pankhurst cannot deny that. They cannot refute the fact that, in the ranks of the Labour Party, the British Socialist Party enjoys sufficient freedom to write that certain leaders of the Labour Party are traitors; that these old leaders represent the interests of the bourgeoisie; that they are agents of the bourgeoisie in the working-class movement. They cannot deny all this because it is the absolute truth. When Communists enjoy such freedom it is their duty to join the Labour Party if they take due account of the experience of revolutionaries in all countries, not only of the Russian revolution (for here we are not at a Russian congress but at one that is international). Comrade Gallacher has said ironically that in the present instance we are under the influence of the British Socialist Party. That is not true; it is the experience of all revolutions in all countries that has convinced us. We think that we must say that to the masses. The British Communist Party must retain the freedom necessary to expose and criticise the betrayers of the working class, who are much more powerful in Britain than in any other country. That is readily understandable. Comrade Gallacher is wrong in asserting that by advocating affiliation to the Labour Party we shall repel the best elements among the British workers. We must test this by experience. We are convinced that all the resolutions and decisions that will be adopted by our Congress will be published in all British revolutionary socialist newspapers and that all the branches and sections will be able to discuss them. The entire content of our resolutions shows with crystal clarity that we are representatives of working-class revolutionary tactics in all countries and that our aim is to fight against the old reformism and opportunism. The events reveal that our tactics are indeed defeating the old reformism. In that case the finest revolutionary elements in the working class, who are dissatisfied with the slow progress being made—and progress in Britain will perhaps be slower than in other countries—will all come over to us. Progress is slow because the British bourgeoisie are in a position to create better conditions for the labour aristocracy and thereby to retard the revolutionary movement in Britain. That is why the British comrades should strive, not only to revolutionise the masses—they are doing that splendidly (as Comrade Gallacher has shown), but must at the same time strive to create a real working-class political party. Comrade Gallacher and

Comrade Sylvia Pankhurst, who have both spoken here, do not as yet belong to a revolutionary Communist Party. That excellent proletarian organization, the Shop Stewards' movement, has not yet joined a political party. If you organise politically you will find that our tactics are based on a correct understanding of political developments in the past decades, and that a real revolutionary party can be created only when it absorbs the best elements of the revolutionary class and uses every opportunity to fight the reactionary leaders, wherever they show themselves.

If the British Communist Party starts by acting in a revolutionary manner in the Labour Party, and if the Hendersons are obliged to expel this Party, that will be a great victory for the communist and revolutionary working class movement in Britain.

Made in the USA
Monee, IL
07 July 2026